LOVE'S VOICE

BOOK 16 LOVE'S MAGIC SERIES

BETTY MCLAIN

This book is dedicated to my family.
They are the ones keeping the voice in my head
around.
I would be unable to use my imagination to bring the
stories;
In my head, to life without the voice.

Mariam Janice Semp - Kindergarten teacher fleeing witch hunters

Darrin Semp – Mariam's brother

Mark Avorn – Darrin's friend

Alex Avorn – Mark's brother – Head and owner of security investigative firm

Darci Holt – Bookstore owner

Charles Holt – Deputy sheriff – Darci's grandson

Stan Varin – Alex's employee

Andrew Salto – Alex's employee

Lori and Trey Loden – Alex's employees

Salvdori Mase (Sal) and Michael Ansel (Micky) – Alex's employees

Brenda – Alex's personal assistant

Woodrow Talcove – Mayor

Lana Talcove – Charles' sister

Sara Talcove – Charles' niece

Kenny Moore – Retired police officer

CHAPTER 1

*D*anger. Hide. Mariam Janice Semp was on the run. Someone wanted her dead. The voice of her guardian angel in her head kept her alive, warning her of dangers. Others weren't so fortunate.

First came the fire that burned down her home, destroyed all she owned, and claimed the lives of her mother, father, and younger brother. Darrin, her older brother, was off serving in the army. She tried to reach him, but he was off base, so all she could do was leave a message. Then came the second attack.

"Danger!" the voice of her guardian angel said, just before a car tried to run her down in the street. She dove and fell out of the way. Any notion it was an accident was dispelled as the driver turned the car to try and hit her a second time, but her roll had landed her safely hidden between two parked cars. Another vehicle drove by, and her attacker sped away.

The next time she heard the voice of her guardian angel, Mariam had seen lights headed toward her and looked back to see the same car. "Hide," the voice instructed. She slid down into a ditch and hid under some branches. The car slowed as it drove past her position. The next time she saw the mysterious car, bidden by the voice, she hid in a tree until it drove away. That time she caught a glimpse of light shining off the metal of a gun barrel. The driver had a gun.

Mariam was afraid to go to the police. She had started to, but the voice of her guardian angel had objected loudly. She didn't know why, but she had learned to listen.

Mariam lived in the town of Madison, Oklahoma, where she was a kindergarten teacher. She decided to try to get as far away from her hometown as she could. She had limited funds. Unless she was able to somehow go by an ATM without being seen, all she had was about three hundred dollars hidden in a false pocket in her jacket. The voice of her guardian angel had advised her to hide the money about a month ago and, even though Mariam had not understood why at the time, she had obeyed.

Mariam went into a grocery store on the other side of town from where she had lived. She saw a sign advertising an ATM. She looked around. When she did not see anyone suspicious, she put her card in the machine and asked for $950.00. The limit for one transaction was $1000.00. She did not want to draw attention to herself by getting the limit. When the money was approved, she turned so people could not see how much money she was getting, Mariam put the money in an inside pocket in her coat. On her way out of the store, she moved forward with a group of shoppers, so she would not stand out. When they were outside, she slipped away from the group and made her way through the shadows to the outskirts of town.

There was a truck stop there, and Mariam hid

and watched the trucks come and go. She watched an older man get out of his truck and go inside. He did not lock his door. She eased over to his truck. Her guardian angel was silent. Miriam eased open the door. She looked around, but she didn't see anyone. The truck was parked where people inside could not see the door.

Mariam crawled inside and eased the door shut. She crawled on into the back and, getting down behind the seat, she pulled a blanket up from the floor and covered herself with it. She had taken the money out of her pocket and stuffed most of it down in her boots. She only kept a couple of twenties in her pocket.

Mariam made herself into as small a ball as she could and lay very still as she heard the driver return. He climbed into his truck. Since he had left it running, all he had to do was start driving. They were on their way. Her guardian angel was being very quiet. Mariam took it to mean there was no danger. Her guardian angel was always loud when she was in danger. Mariam lay under the blanket and fell asleep. They were a long way down the road before she awoke. The man in the truck had stopped and was putting gas in the truck.

Mariam saw him when she eased up and peeped out the window. The man had finished pumping gas and was on his way inside the store. Mariam had no idea where she was. She looked at the clock in the dashboard. It said 11:30.

She had been asleep for 7 hours. She looked at the sign on the store. It said, "Mercy Truck Stop." Mariam climbed up and eased out of the truck. She saw the truck driver come out of the store and ran around the back of the truck to hide behind the building. She heard the driver get in his truck and drive away.

Mariam looked around the side of the building. She had never heard of the town of Mercy. She had left the truck here because the voice of her guardian angel had been so silent. She had been so vocal for so long; the silence was a relief. With a name like Mercy, maybe she would be safe. She needed to find a place to stay until morning. She could look around then and see what she could do. She looked around and spotted a storage shed just inside the trees. She didn't see anyone around, so she hurried over to the building. It wasn't locked. Mariam opened the door and looked inside. It had furniture stored in it. It was very dark inside, so Mariam left the door open a little so she could look around. There was a chair and a couple of sofas. She could curl up on one of the sofas to wait for morning. Only, Mariam wasn't sleepy; she was hungry and needed a bathroom.

"Maybe if I act natural, I can go in the store and buy something to eat and get the key to the bathroom. If I go in from this side, the clerk will think I am parked around this side of the building," said Mariam.

She straightened her clothes and smoothed her hair and headed for the store. When she went in, the clerk barely glanced at her. She picked out some snacks and paid for them.

"Could I get the key to the restroom?" asked Mariam.

The clerk reached up and snagged the key off a hook and handed it to her.

"The restroom is around back," said the clerk.

"Thanks," said Mariam.

She went around back and used the restroom. When she had finished and washed her hands, she left the door unlocked and took the key back to the clerk. He took it silently and hung it back up. Hopefully, no one else would come along and re-lock it, thought Mariam.

She went back to the storage shed, went inside and, made herself comfortable on one of the sofas. She opened one of her snacks and enjoyed the first food she had eaten all day. It tasted very good.

When Mariam awoke the next morning, she looked out a crack in the door to be sure no one was around. When she didn't see anyone, she hurried over to the restroom.

After using the restroom and washing her hands, she used a small comb from her pocket to smooth down her hair. Having short hair helped a lot. Mariam came out of the restroom and headed for the town. She could see the buildings a couple of blocks away.

When she entered the town, she found it was built in a circle around a small park. The park had small tables with a bench attached on each side like picnic tables. It looked like what would be put out for older men to sit at and play checkers.

Mariam looked across the park and saw a café. Her stomach picked that moment to growl very loudly. It was ready to eat.

Mariam headed for the café across the way. Mariam looked around curiously. She spotted an empty table and headed for it. As soon as she sat down, a waitress appeared with a glass of water and a menu.

"Hi, I'm Sue. What can I get for you?"

Mariam looked at the menu. "I'll have the breakfast platter with orange juice and coffee," said Mariam.

The waitress took the menu and went to turn in the order. There were only a few people there. They were all watching her. They were curious about the stranger in their small town.

The waitress was soon back with her food and orange juice.

"I'll be right back with your coffee," said Sue.

Mariam just nodded and started eating. She had to force herself to eat slowly. She was so hungry; she was afraid she would eat too fast and embarrass herself. The food was delicious. Mariam didn't know if it was just because she was so hungry, but she couldn't remember food ever tasting so good.

When Mariam's hunger was under control, she looked around. There were two ladies sitting at a table across from her. They were eating and talking and sneaking glances at her. Mariam smiled at them, and they smiled back and turned their attention back to their meal.

There was a man at another table, sitting by himself. He grinned and looked down when he saw the ladies look away, embarrassed at being caught staring. The man finished his meal and left some money on the table as he went up front to pay his bill. He glanced at Mariam and grinned as he left.

Mariam watched him leave, but she didn't smile back. She was still being cautious. She did not know who was trying to kill her. She should be safe here, but she was not taking anything for granted.

When Mariam finished and paid her bill, she went out and looked up and down the street. She decided to go to her right and make a circle around the town. As she went down the street, she passed a drug store and a furniture store. Next was the jail. Mariam saw the man from the café going in the door. After the jail was a hardware store.

Mariam paused and glanced through the window. It looked like a nice place and seemed to be doing a good business. Looking in the hardware store window made Mariam think about her family. Her dad had worked in the hardware store in Madison. She sighed, feeling depressed, then continued on her way.

Mariam came to the circle at the end of the street. The courthouse was sitting back away from the street. It had a large parking area around it. It had large columns out front. On down from the courthouse was a fire station. The doors were closed, and there did not seem to be anyone around.

Mariam continued her journey of discovery. After the fire station, Mariam gazed in delight at a bookstore. It had a help wanted sign in the window. The store wasn't open yet, so Mariam went on to see the rest of the stores. There was another café next, and a grocery store. They were followed by an antique store. The antique store had some of its merchandise displayed on the sidewalk in front of the store. There was a resale clothing store next. Mariam took notice of it because all her clothes had been lost in the fire. All she had to wear was what she had on. She did not want to spend a lot of money on clothes. The resale store might be an answer for her.

Mariam turned and headed back to the bookstore to inquire about the job. The store was open when she arrived at the door. When she went in, an elderly lady was sitting behind the cash register working on a ledger.

The woman smiled at Mariam and looked at her closely. "Come on in," she said cheerfully.

"Hi," said Mariam. "I saw your sign in the window. I was wondering about the job."

"Have you had any experience working in a bookstore?" asked the lady.

"Not in sales," said Mariam. "but I have helped out in the school library."

"Were you a teacher?" asked the lady.

Mariam nodded. "I taught kindergarten."

"Why did you stop teaching?" she asked.

"My family was killed in a house fire. I lost everything, and I needed to get away," remarked Mariam.

"I'm sorry," said the woman studying her. "My name is Darci Holt. What's your name, dear?"

"I'm Mariam Janice," said Mariam. She left her last name off. Maybe it would throw off anyone looking for her.

Darci nodded and looked around thoughtfully. "Where are you staying, Mariam?"

"I haven't found a place yet. I thought I would try to find work first and then look for a place to stay," said Mariam.

"I have a room in the back of the store. It is just one large room and a bath. It has a microwave and a small refrigerator. You can stay there while you look around," said Darci.

"You mean I have the job?" asked Mariam smiling.

"Yes," said Darci. "I should tell you before you

take the job, some people around here seem to think I am a witch."

"Why would they think that?" asked Mariam startled.

"They found out about my hearing the voice of my guardian angel. If it wasn't for my grandson, they would probably have run me out of town. He is a deputy sheriff. They don't want to get on his bad side. You don't seem surprised about me hearing my guardian angel," observed Darci.

Mariam shook her head. "I hear the voice of my guardian angel, too," she said.

Darci nodded. "I know you do. My guardian angel told me to help you. She said you are in danger because of your guardian angel's voice," she said.

"I didn't know it was because of the voice," said Mariam. "My family was killed because of me," said Mariam, looking away to hide her tears.

Darci came around the counter and put her arm around Mariam's shoulder. "It was not because of you. It was the witch hunters. They think they have the right to take life when they want to. They need to be stopped. My grandson is working on it. It takes time to build a case against them. If it is not done legally, it makes us as bad as them. Now, do you want the job?"

"Yes, I do," said Mariam.

"Come on back, and I will show you your room. You can go down to the resale store and pick up a couple of outfits. You can start to work after lunch. I'll help you get acquainted with how I do things around here," said Darci as she guided Mariam to the back of the store and showed her the room. She gave her the key to her room and went back to the front because the bell rang when a customer entered the store.

Mariam looked around the room. It had everything she needed. She was inside, warm, had a cozy place to sleep and a place to eat and shower.

Mariam took some of the money from her boots and added it to the money in her hidden pocket. She put some in her pocket and some in her wallet. Mariam decided to go and find some clothes before she showered. She could also pick up a few groceries. The refrigerator was running but empty. Mariam went out and locked her door. She smiled at Darci as she went through the bookstore on her way to the stores. Darci smiled at her and nodded.

The customer turned and looked at Mariam. "Who is she?" the customer leaned in to ask.

"Her name is Mariam, and she is my new helper," Darci answered casually. The woman nodded, accepting the information, and Mariam breathed a sigh of relief. The door closed behind her, blocking out the rest of their exchange.

Mariam continued to the resale store. After finding a couple of pairs of jeans and three shirts, she found some underwear and socks. The underwear was still in its original unopened packages. Mariam paid for her clothes and headed for the grocery store. She put her clothes in the buggy and started around the store. She couldn't buy much. She was walking and didn't want to be overloaded.

Mariam picked up a box of cereal and a half-gallon of milk. She could go to the café after work, but she needed something for breakfast before work. Mariam picked up a couple of bags of microwave popcorn. It would make a tasty snack.

Mariam paid for her purchases and left the grocery store. She carried her purchases in her arms and headed for the bookstore. Darci was busy when Mariam entered the bookstore. She smiled as she took in Mariam's load. Mariam smiled and headed for her room. She wanted to take a shower and change clothes before she started working.

Word had reached Charles Holt about Darci having a new helper. He decided to drop by and check on his grandmother. He wanted to be sure no one was taking advantage of her. Although she was a very smart lady and her guardian angel warned her about danger, he still felt he should take care of her.

Charles entered the bookstore and saw his grandmother finishing with a customer. She handed the lady her package and receipt. The customer took her package, smiled, and nodded at Charles as she left.

Darci smiled and came over and let Charles kiss her cheek. "Hello, Charles, I see the grapevine is working well.".

Charles laughed. "I hear you have a new helper," he said.

"Yes, her name is Mariam Janice. She is starting this afternoon, and I am letting her use the room in the back of the store," said Darci.

Charles looked at her sharply. "Why did you let her stay in the store?" he asked.

"She was new in town and needed a place to stay." She looked at him sternly. "My guardian angel told me to help her," said Darci.

Charles shook his head. There was no arguing

with her guardian angel. If her angel told her it was what she should do, no one was going to change Darci's mind. He would just have to keep an eye on the situation and make sure she was not taken advantage of.

"Alright, Grandma, I will see you later. If you need me, call," said Charles. He gave her a hug as he turned and left the store to return to the station.

CHAPTER 2

In the town of Madison, Darrin Semp was trying to find out what had happened to his sister. He had asked for leave from the army and was granted a week. He buried his mother, dad, and little brother, but no one could tell him where his sister, Mariam, was. The police gave him no help. They couldn't tell him why his home had been burned down with his family in it. They acted unconcerned about the whereabouts of Mariam. It was as if his sister had vanished after leaving him the message about the fire.

He was very worried. He knew his sister would have been at the funeral if she could have. There had to be something keeping her away. Darrin was stumped. He didn't know what to do. How was he supposed to go about finding a grown woman when the police refused to even look for her?

Darrin went to the room he had taken at a local motel. He called his friend at the base.

"Hi, Mark, I need some advice," said Darrin when Mark answered his phone.

"Hi, how did the funeral go?" asked Mark.

"It went okay. My sister Mariam has still not shown up. The police are not interested in helping me. They are not even trying to find out who burned our house and killed my family," said Darrin.

"What can I do to help?" asked Mark.

"I only have a couple more days of leave. I was wondering if your brother Alex might be able to help me," said Darrin.

"I don't know how busy he is, but I will call him and call you back," said Mark.

"Thanks," said Darrin.

They hung up. A minute later, the phone rang back with Mark's brother on the line.

"Hello, Darrin, Mark told me what was going on. I'm sorry about your folks and brother," said Alex.

"Thanks," said Darrin. "Do you think you can help me? I am worried sick about my sister."

"I don't know if I can find her, but I will try. Mark said you have two more days of leave. Give me the address where you are staying, and I will be there first thing in the morning. We will talk and see what needs to be done," said Alex.

"I'm at the Econo motel on the edge of town. Thank you, Alex," said Darrin.

They hung up, and Darrin experienced his first breath of hope since he had heard the news of the fire.

Alex pulled into the Econo motel at seven the next morning. He didn't have to worry about waking Darrin. He had been sleeping very little since he had received the phone call from his sister. When Alex knocked on the door, Darrin opened at once.

"Thanks for coming, Alex," said Darrin. "I have tried talking to everyone Mariam knows. No one will tell me anything."

Alex came in and shook Darrin's hand. "I can't make you any promises, but I will see if I can help." He took his laptop over to a table and set it on the table. He sat in the chair and opened it up. "Do you have a current picture of your sister?"

"Yes," said Darrin. He took a picture of Mariam out of his wallet and handed it to Alex. Alex studied the picture. "Do you know if she has a bank account?"

"Yes, she has an account at First State," said Darrin. "I don't know her social security number."

"Do you have her phone number?" asked Alex.

"Yes," said Darrin. "She hasn't answered it since I have been trying to call her after she left me the message about the fire. Her car was in the garage at home. It burned with the house." He gave Alex the phone number.

Alex started working on his computer. In just a few minutes, he pulled up the information about Mariam drawing $950.00 out of the ATM at the grocery store. Alex showed the information to Darrin.

"This grocery store is on the other side of town. We never shop there," said Darrin.

Alex closed his computer. "Let's go see if we can look at their security footage." He and Darrin went out to his car, and Darrin gave him directions to the grocery store.

They went into the store and went upstairs to the security office. Alex showed the man in the security office his credentials and explained about Mariam being missing. "We want to look at the security footage for the time when she visited the ATM. We want to be sure someone else wasn't using her card or forcing her to get money out for them," said Alex.

Alex gave the man the time of the withdrawal,

and he looked through the tapes and found the correct one. He put the tape in a player, and Alex and Darrin stood with him as they all studied the tape.

"There she is," said Darrin.

They watched as Mariam looked around before going to the ATM. They watched her as she withdrew the money and as she shielded the cash so no one could see how much she was getting. They saw her put the money in an inside pocket of her coat. They watched her blend in with some other customers and make her way out of the store.

"Look how she keeps glancing around. She looks scared to death," said Darrin.

Alex turned to the security man. "Do you have footage of the outside?"

The security man went over and selected another tape. He brought it over and prepared to play it. "You guys are lucky. Another day and these tapes would have been erased. We don't keep them very long," he said.

When the tape of the outside started playing, they watched Mariam come out with the group. They saw her look around and then blend into the shadows and fade away.

Alex shook the security man's hand. "Thank you for showing the tapes to us. You said they would be erased. Could we buy the tapes from you and then you can start out with new tapes; no one would know the difference, and if anyone comes asking about them you could just tell them they are gone. They will think they have been erased."

He took a hundred dollar bill out and held it out to the security man. The man handed them the two tapes and a bag to put them in and took the bill.

Darrin and Alex went back to Darrin's motel room and looked over the tapes again. They studied them closely and decided Mariam was scared and trying not to be seen. They decided to follow the road in the direction Mariam had been heading when she left the grocery store. They drove down the road. They passed the truck stop, but decided not to go in and ask questions.

They decided if Mariam had been in trouble and was trying to get away, they would risk drawing attention to her. They did not want to put her in danger. Darrin tried to call her phone again, but it went straight to voice mail. He left a message for Mariam to call him but did not say anything else.

When they returned to the motel, Alex called Mark and told him he was going to try and find Darrin's sister. Mark wished him luck. Darrin spoke to Mark and thanked him for sending Alex to help.

Alex decided he needed to look over the place where Darrin's family house had been burned. There was police tape around the burned area. But they ignored it. After looking over the area, Alex stopped and looked thoughtful.

"It looks like someone poured gasoline around the outside of the house and the garage. I think they broke in and doused the downstairs also, probably after everyone was upstairs asleep. They started the fire downstairs, then went outside and set the fire to burning out there. Since Mariam's car was in the garage, they may have thought she was upstairs sleeping, too," said Alex. "Why didn't she take her car?"

"I spoke to her friend, Jenny. She said Mariam was having trouble with her brakes. She was supposed to take it to the repair shop the next day. Jenny picked her up, and they went to the mall. Jenny ran into a boyfriend, and Mariam took a cab home. Jenny hasn't heard from her since," said Darrin.

Alex looked at Darrin. "I'll need Jenny's name and telephone number and the name of the cab company she used."

Darrin nodded. He wrote down the requested information and gave it to Alex. Alex seemed to be just driving around, but he ended back at the truck stop. He pulled in and stopped. He looked at Darrin.

"We are going to order coffee. Let me do the talking. We are not going to mention Mariam. I don't want to alert anyone who might be looking for her," said Alex.

"Okay," agreed Darrin as he followed Alex inside the truck stop. They ordered coffee and took it over and sat at a table close to some truckers. The truckers were eating and talking. They acted like they were friends. They were laughing and talking – swapping stories.

Alex and Darrin listened to them talking for a while before Alex decided to speak. He smiled at one of the truckers, who looked at him. "It must be exciting driving around seeing the country," he said.

The trucker smiled back at Alex. "Most of us have regular routes. We drive the same way on each trip. We are used to the scenery on our trips," he said.

"Bummer," said Alex. "It would get old driving the same way all of the time."

"It gets old, but it does pay well," said one of the truckers.

They all laughingly agreed.

"What are you guys doing in a truck stop?" asked one of the truckers.

Alex grinned. "My mom was a trucker. She always said if I wanted good food or company, the best place to go was a truck stop. We were just driving around looking and spotted the truck stop and decided to stop and get a cup of coffee."

"Your mom was right," said the older trucker. "The food is good, and you won't meet a better group of people anywhere."

All the truckers nodded in agreement. "I thought about going to driving school when I finished my enlistment, but I decided it was too much driving," said Alex.

"What service were you in?" asked one of the older truckers.

"I was in the army," answered Alex.

"Are you from around here?" asked the first trucker.

"No, I came to be with my friend here. His family was killed in a house fire, and I didn't want him to have to go through the funeral alone," said Alex.

"I am sorry for your loss," the trucker said to Darrin.

"Thank you," said Darrin with a nod.

"Hey, I heard about the fire. I was here a few days ago on my way to Kansas, and all they could talk about was the fire," said an older trucker. He left a tip on the table and prepared to leave.

"I will see you guys on my next trip to Mercy," he said to his companions.

"Mercy," repeated Alex.

"Mercy, Kansas. It's where I make most of my deliveries," he said.

Alex smiled and nodded. Alex and Darrin finished their coffee, and telling the truckers to have a nice trip, they went back to the motel.

When they were back at the motel, Alex called his office. He had asked his assistant to find out all she could about Mariam Janis Semp.

When he hung up his phone, he turned to Darrin.

"I have Mariam's social security number. Her phone has not been used since she called you. There are a lot of messages from you and several hang-ups. There was one message left before the hang-ups. It was from the same number. It said, "We will get you, witch. You can't escape.""

Darrin turned pale. He sat down on the side of the bed.

"It's why she is so scared. Someone is trying to kill her," he said.

"Why do they think she is a witch?" asked Alex.

Darrin looked at Alex sharply. "My sister is not a witch."

"I didn't say she was. I asked why they think she is," said Alex.

"Mariam sometimes hears the voice of her guardian angel in her head. It warns her of danger. We haven't told anyone about it because we wanted to protect her from the witch hunters. Mom had an aunt who heard voices, and she was stoned to death by the witch hunters. Since then, we have kept quiet about Mariam hearing the voice of her guardian angel," said Darrin.

Alex nodded and looked thoughtful.

"Someone must have found out and alerted the hunters. They burned your family home, trying to get to Mariam. Now, they are trying to find her," said Alex.

"How are we going to find her without leading the witch hunters to her?" asked Darrin.

"You are going back to the base and leaving the hunting to me. I will do a little more looking around here. Then, I will leave. I don't think she is here anymore," said Alex. "I am not going to stay long. I want to talk to her friend Jenny. If she doesn't use her social security number or phone or draw any money from the bank, she should be safe."

Darrin looked at Alex and nodded.

"You do believe my sister is not a witch?" he asked.

"I believe you," said Alex. "This isn't the first time I've heard of the witch hunters. I have seen what destruction they can do. I think your sister was smart not going to the police for help. They probably have people on the police force. That is why they would not help you. It also makes it harder to keep them from finding her because they have the police resources to help them."

Darrin shook his head and looked defeated.

Alex stood and put a hand on Darrin's shoulder. "We will find her. Don't give up. When you are back on base, I will call my reports to you through Mark. They may have your phone bugged. We don't want to give them any information they don't already have," said Alex.

"Okay," agreed Darrin. "Thanks for helping and believing me about Mariam."

Alex shook Darrin's hand and walked out of the room with him as he took his duffle bag and put it in the back seat of his rental car and started on his trip back to base. Alex stood looking after Darrin for a minute. He saw a car start up and follow Darrin out of town.

Alex took out his phone and called his office. "Brenda," he said when his assistant answered the phone. "Is Stan around? Let me talk to him."

"Hello," said Stan.

"Stan, my new client, Darrin Semp, just left on his way back to base. He was followed. I want you to see if you can intersect with him and make sure he gets back to base all right. Keep an eye on him for a while and make sure he doesn't end up like his family," said Alex.

"Sure thing, Boss, do you want one of the others to come and help?" asked Stan.

"Not yet," said Alex. "I'll do a bit more looking around, and then I will decide," said Alex.

They both hung up, and Stan went to look after Darrin. Alex went to find and talk to Jenny.

CHAPTER 3

Things were going well for Mariam in Mercy, Kansas. She loved working in the bookstore, and she loved helping the younger children find books to read. Darci encouraged her to start a reading group with the younger children.

Darci and the children's parents stood and listened when Mariam read for the children. As time passed, the people in town came to accept Mariam's presence after seeing how well she interacted with the children.

Deputy Charles Holt, Darci's grandson, had stopped by several times, but he had not talked to Mariam yet. He was just checking on his grandma. He relaxed some after seeing how well Mariam was fitting in. Also, he had put the name Mariam Janice through the system at the police station, and the report come back with no red flags.

Mariam was still nervous around him and avoided him when she saw him enter the bookstore. Darci would smile when she saw Mariam head the other way whenever Charles was around. She did not say anything. She decided to let time take care of things.

"Hello," said Charles.

Mariam jumped. She had not noticed Charles being in the store.

"Hello," replied Mariam turned away slightly to continue sorting books and putting them on the shelf.

"I didn't mean to startle you," said Charles.

"I just didn't know you were there," replied Mariam.

"How do you like our small town?" asked Charles.

"I like it. Everyone has been very nice to me," said Mariam.

"My grandma says you are a natural in the bookstore. The last helper she had only lasted one day. Grandma said the girl could hardly read and didn't like being around books." Charles chuckled. "Grandma said she couldn't understand why she had tried to work in a bookstore."

Mariam nodded but continued to work.

"Well," said Charles. "I guess I should quit bothering you and let you get on with your work."

Mariam looked up, startled. "I'm sorry. I didn't mean to be rude. You are not bothering me. I guess I just get nervous around police officers. I don't know why. I'm sure you are a very nice person. You take great care of Darci. She always speaks highly of you." Mariam paused and took a deep breath. "Now I can't stop rambling."

Charles smiled. "I don't mind," he said. "It's better than the silent treatment."

Mariam flushed slightly. "I had better get back to work."

"I'll see you later," said Charles.

Mariam nodded and watched him as he went to

talk to Darci. Mariam smiled to herself as she turned away and went back to work.

"Hello, Charles," said Darci. "I see you finally managed to corner Mariam."

Charles looked up sharply. "I wasn't trying to corner her. I was just saying hello."

Darci laughed. "If you say so," she replied.

Charles ignored her remark. "Do you think Mariam will stay here in Mercy?" asked Charles.

Darci looked up at Charles. She was no longer laughing. "I think she would like to stay here. She fits in well with the people and the town. It all depends on whether she feels safe here," said Darci.

"If she starts acting like she doesn't think she is safe, let me know. If anyone bothers her, I will take care of them," said Charles.

Darci patted his hand and smiled. "I'll keep watch. If I get even a hint of those witch hunters, I will let you know at once," agreed Darci.

"Thanks, you stay safe, too. I don't want anything to happen to either of you," said Charles, giving Darci a hug and leaving to go back to work.

Darci watched him go and smiled. She was very proud of that young man. It was a blessing to have him there to watch her back and keep those witch hunters away.

Mariam watched Charles leave and turned to find Darci watching her. She smiled at Darci and made her way over to where Darci was helping a customer. She waited patiently while the older woman rang up the sale and bid the customer goodbye.

"Would it be alright if I leave for lunch, now?" asked Mariam.

"Sure, we are not very busy," said Darci.

"I won't be very long. I just need to stop by the drug store," said Mariam. "I need to pick up a burner phone so I can call my brother. I haven't wanted to call on my phone. I was afraid it could be traced."

"Do you have someone you could call who could give your brother a message? They may have his phone number tagged, too," said Darci.

Mariam thought for a minute. "I could call his friend Mark. They are in the same regiment. Mark could let him know I am alright," said Mariam.

"Why don't you use my phone to call Mark?" said Darci.

Mariam shook her head. "I don't want to do anything to bring you to their attention," said Mariam. "Charles would be very upset if I caused any harm to come to you."

"Charles would be upset if any harm came to you," said Darci.

Mariam smiled. "I'll be back soon."

"Take your time and be sure to eat while you are out," ordered Darci.

"Yes, Ma'am," said Mariam with a smile.

Darci watched her go with a smile. She was becoming very fond of Mariam. She hoped Charles managed to draw her attention. It would be great to have her as a permanent member of her family.

Mariam went to the drug store and looked over the pre-paid phones. She picked out one and bought a card with minutes to use with the phone.

Mariam picked up some food to take back to her room. She looked in her address book and found Mark's phone number to call and let Darrin know she was okay.

"Hello," said Mark Avorn.

"Hello, Mark, this is Mariam Semp. I'm Darrin's sister."

"Mariam, Darrin has been trying to find you. He has been worried sick about you," said Mark.

"I know, I'm sorry. I couldn't use my phone. I was afraid it could be traced. I have a burner phone. I'm calling you so you can let Darrin know I am alright. I thought the witch hunters may have his phone tagged, too," said Mariam.

"Where are you?" asked Mark.

"It's better if you don't know. Will you please tell Darrin I'm alright and I will try to keep in touch with him through you? The witch hunters tried to kill me three times, four if you count burning our house," said Mariam.

"I wish Darrin was here," said Mark. "He would feel better if he could talk to you."

"Where is he?" asked Mariam.

"He is out on patrol. He stayed a few days after the funeral to talk to my brother Alex about finding you, and the officers have him doing extra patrols since he returned," said Mark.

"Your brother is a private detective, isn't he?" asked Mariam.

"Yes, he is," said Mark. "When Darrin could not get any help from the police, he asked Alex to help find out what happened to you."

"Please tell Darrin to stop looking for me. He could lead the witch hunters to me," begged Mariam.

"I'll see what I can do. My brother, Alex, is very good at what he does. He would not put you in danger," said Mark.

"He might not mean to, but there are a lot of people working with the witch hunters. He can't trust the police. They are spotters for the witch hunters," said Mariam. "I have to go. Tell Darrin I love him, and I will be in touch when I can. I am going to have this phone turned off, so he can't call me on it."

"I'll tell him. If you need help, call Alex. You can trust him to keep you safe," said Mark. He gave her Alex's number and, after telling her to stay safe, they hung up.

Mariam started to eat her food. She didn't really feel hungry, but she knew Darci would ask her if she had eaten. She was misty-eyed. Talking to Mark had made her think about her parents and little brother. Thanks to the witch hunters, she had missed saying goodbye to them.

Mariam brushed her tears away and thought about Darrin. The best thing she could do for him was to stay away. If he was around her, the witch hunters may try to kill him, too.

Mariam finished what food she could eat and put the rest in the refrigerator for later. She cleaned up and went to the bookstore to work.

Darci saw her come in and smiled as Mariam made her way over to her. "Did you call your brother's friend?"

"Yes," said Mariam, nodding. "Mark is going to tell Darrin I am alright. He said Darrin had asked Mark's brother, Alex, to help find me. Alex is in private security. I told him to ask Darrin to stop him from looking. I don't want them to lead anyone to me."

"Do you think he will listen?" asked Darci.

"I don't know. I am telling you about Alex, in case he does find me, so you will know he is one of the good guys. He can be trusted," said Mariam.

"You can trust Charles, too," said Darci. "He has been looking out for me for years. He would never betray you to the witch hunters."

"I know," said Mariam. "My guardian angel has been so quiet since I came to Mercy; I am beginning to think maybe the whole town is blessed."

Darci laughed. "We have bad ones, just like any other town, but they stay away from me and my store. They don't want to tangle with Charles."

Mariam laughed. "I'm glad he is on our side," she said.

"So am I. Charles has been a blessing for me for years. Just knowing he was out there has made me feel safer," said Darci.

"You said you hear your guardian angel, too. Has she been extra quiet lately?" asked Mariam.

Darci looked up quickly. She was startled. "I haven't thought about it, but my guardian angel has been quiet since you arrived and she told me to help you," said Darci. "I guess she is satisfied with me doing what she wanted."

Mariam smiled. "I am glad you listened to her. I have loved being here. I haven't felt such peace in a long time," said Mariam. "I hope you don't mind me staying in the room in back. When you offered it to me, you said it was temporary until I found somewhere else."

"You can stay there as long as you want," assured Darci. "I was afraid it would be too small for you."

"It is fine," said Mariam. "I love the room. It's perfect for me." Mariam looked at Darci seriously. "It is such a relief to be able to talk about the voice of my guardian angel. All my life, my mom had told me and my brothers not to let anyone know about hearing them. She had an aunt who could hear the voice of her guardian angel. Her parents thought she was crazy and locked her away when she was younger. Mom was afraid the same thing would happen to us. To actually meet someone who can hear her guardian angel and be able to talk about it is an amazing feeling."

Darci nodded. "I know what you mean. Several people in my family could hear the voices of their guardian angels. We were all warned not to let anyone know. At least we could talk to each other. It became harder when the witch hunters showed up. We became afraid to talk about our guardian angels, even among ourselves. Having Charles look out for me has been a blessing."

Mariam and Darci looked out the window and saw some little ones headed their way with their mothers.

"Do you have a reading for the little ones today?" asked Darci.

"If enough show up, I'll gather them around and read to them," agreed Mariam.

"Do you think we should put out some cookies for them?" asked Darci.

"I don't think so, not unless you give them a cookie as they are leaving. We don't want crumbs all over the books," said Mariam.

Darci smiled. I think I will put a cookie in a plastic bag and give it to them as they are leaving."

"Okay, do you want me to get them ready so you can hand them out?" asked Mariam.

"I'll get them ready if you will watch the front for me," said Darci.

"Sure," said Mariam with a smile. "After all, it is my job."

Darci laughed and left to go and get the cookies and some small bags.

Mariam turned to greet her customers. The little ones started smiling as soon as they spotted Mariam. They ran to her shouting, "Miss Janice, Miss Janice!"

Mariam hugged them back as they hugged her legs.

"Hello, how are my little munchkins this morning?" asked Mariam.

"We are good," replied Sara, one of the more talkative young ones. "Are you going to read to us today?"

"I will, but let's wait a little and see if more children come. Why don't you let your moms help you find books to take home with you while you are waiting," suggested Mariam.

The moms smilingly guided the little ones over to the children's book section.

Mariam turned to check out a customer while keeping an eye on the young children. Even with their moms there with them, they could slip away when their moms were distracted.

While Sara's mom was talking to another mom, Sara turned and went down another row. Mariam followed and kept an eye on Sara. When Sara reached the end of the row and started down another row, Mariam stepped out in front of her. Mariam pretended to be surprised to see Sara.

"Hello, Sara, do you need help?" asked Mariam.

"Hi, Miss Janice, I was just looking around," said Sara. "I need to go find my mom now."

"Come with me, I'll show you the way," said Mariam holding out a hand for Sara to take. With Sara's hand in hers, she headed back to the children's section.

Mariam found Charles standing in the front, grinning at her.

"Hello, Uncle Charles," said Sara.

"Hello, Sara. Are you here to listen to a story?" asked Charles.

Sara nodded. "Just as soon as some more kids show up," said Sara.

Charles smiled and nodded toward Sara's mom. She had just discovered Sara gone and was looking for her. She hurried over to them.

Charles smiled and kissed her on her cheek.

"Hello, Lana; missing someone?" laughed Charles.

"I shouldn't be surprised," said Lana. "I can't take my eye off of her for a minute."

She took Sara's hand and headed back to the group.

Mariam nodded at Charles. "Darci will be back in a few minutes. She went to get some cookies for the children."

Charles laughed. "She is going to have the store flooded with little ones if she keeps spoiling them."

Mariam grinned. "It's good for business. If the children have good experiences in the bookstore while they are young, they will become lifelong customers."

"You may be right," agreed Charles thoughtfully.

Mariam nodded. "Does it surprise you that I may be right?" asked Mariam.

Charles raised his hands as if in surrender. "I have no doubt you are right about a lot of things," he said.

Mariam grinned. "I was just teasing you," she said.

"Will you have dinner with me tonight?" asked Charles.

Mariam looked at him sharply. "Where did that come from?" she asked.

"I have wanted to ask you, but I thought you would say it was too soon and turn me down," said Charles.

Mariam was nodding her head in agreement. "It is too soon," she said.

"It's just a meal. I promise to take good care of you and get you home safe and sound," said Charles.

Mariam stood thinking about it.

"Say 'please,' Uncle Charles," said Sara, who had silently joined them.

"Please," said Charles.

Mariam smiled at Sara. "Okay," she said.

"Please always works," said Sara with satisfaction.

Charles smiled at her. Charles left while Mariam prepared to join the group entering with the group already there for a reading.

Darci hurried in with the bags of cookies, and Mariam gathered the little ones into a group to tell them a story about the little engine that could.

CHAPTER 4

$\mathcal{A}$lex was on his way back to his office. Jenny turned out to be a dead end. She had no idea where Mariam was or why she had left. Alex could tell Jenny was unaware of Mariam hearing the voice of her guardian angel. For a friend, she seemed very unconcerned about Mariam's disappearance.

Brenda met Alex when he entered his office.

"I have the report on Mariam Janice Semp," said Brenda.

Alex took the report from her and went to sit at his desk.

"Have you heard anything from Stan?" asked Alex.

"Yes, he called in. Darrin Semp arrived at base, and the car following him drove away when they saw him entering the base," said Brenda. "Stan said he was going to hang around for a while to be sure the guys in the car don't come back."

"Guys," repeated Alex. "There was more than one?"

"Stan said there were two," said Brenda.

"Was there anything interesting in the report?" asked Alex.

"Well, there was a request for information from a small town in Kansas. A Deputy Sheriff wanted to know if there were any warrants out for a Mariam Janice," said Brenda. "I thought it was an interesting coincidence."

"It may be the name she is using. Where in Kansas?" asked Alex.

"A small town called Mercy," replied Brenda.

Alex sat up straight, looking startled. "One of the truckers said he made regular trips to Mercy, Kansas," said Alex.

"Do you think it could be her?" asked Brenda.

"Yes, I do. I just hope no one else picks up on it. If the hunters find out where she is, she could be in serious trouble," said Alex. "I am going to the penthouse to switch my clothes. I want you to find out the closest airport to Mercy, Kansas, and book me a flight to it. Call me on my cell phone and let me know when my flight is scheduled. Also, arrange for a car rental. Get in touch with Andrew. Tell him to join me there as soon as he wraps up the case he is on."

Alex was giving instructions as he walked out the door and down the hall. Brenda was walking with him, writing down his instructions.

"Anything else?" she asked as Alex entered the elevator.

"If I think of anything else, I will call," said Alex as he grinned at Brenda. "Thanks, Brenda." The door to the elevator closed between them.

Brenda smiled and turned back to her office to get busy.

~

Darrin had no clue about the car or Stan following him back to base. Mark hurried over to him as soon as he spotted him come in from his patrol.

"Mariam called me," said Mark quietly. "It was just a couple of hours ago. She said she is fine, but she is hiding from the witch hunters. She was on a burner phone. She was afraid to use hers, and she didn't want to call yours. She said she will try to call me again so you will know she is alright, but she is going to keep the phone off, so you won't be able to call her."

"She really is okay," said Darrin with relief. "Did she say where she is?"

"She said it would be safer if you don't know. She said the witch hunters had tried to kill her four times, counting the house fire," said Mark.

Darrin cursed softly and turned and looked away.

"You need to call Alex and let him know she called," said Darrin.

Darrin looked around. "Let's go to the locker room where we won't be overheard," said Darrin. He and Mark went to Darrin's locker to pick up a change of clothes and a towel to take with them to the locker room.

Once inside, they checked the room to be sure no one was there. Darrin went to take a shower, and Mark took out his phone to call Alex.

Alex was in the penthouse when his phone rang.

"Hi, Alex, Darrin told me to call you and let you know Mariam called me. She wanted me to let Darrin know she is alright. She is hiding from the witch hunters. They tried to kill her four times in Madison, once when they burned her family home. She wouldn't tell me where she was, and she called on a burner phone. She said she was going to keep it turned off, so it won't do any good to call it."

"Thanks for letting me know. Tell Darrin I won't lead the hunters to her, but I have a lead on where she is. I'm going to make sure she stays safe. I will keep in touch through you, and you can call Brenda to forward any information you get to me. Try to keep Darrin from going off the deep end. He needs a good friend right now," said Alex.

"I'll do my best. Thanks for helping, Alex," said Mark.

"You're welcome, take care, little brother," said Alex.

They hung up the phone, and Alex went to take a shower and get ready for his flight to Mercy. Mark sat back to wait on Darrin.

When Darrin came out of the shower and prepared to shave, Mark was waiting with a report from Alex.

"He said to tell you he would not lead the witch hunters to Mariam, but he has a lead on where she is, and he is going to make sure she stays safe," said Mark.

Darrin looked at Mark and sighed. "I wish I could see for myself. I would feel a lot better if I could talk to her."

"I know," said Mark. "But you don't want to put her in danger. Let Alex handle it. He will keep her safe. He knows what to do."

"I know," said Darrin with a sigh.

Darrin finished shaving and dressing, and the two of them went out into the barracks to head for the mess hall for a meal. Darrin tried to be calm and appear relaxed, but Mariam was always at the front of his mind.

Darrin wondered how long it would be before they shipped out. He hated the idea of being on the other side of the world when his sister was in danger. There was nothing he could do about it. He had another year to go before he could be discharged. He had been thinking about reenlisting and making the service his life, but with his parent's death, he could not leave Mariam to deal with the witch hunters alone. He was just hoping she could stay safe for the next year.

Brenda managed to contact Andrew. He was already finished with his case and would meet Alex in Mercy, Kansas. Brenda booked both Alex and Andrew into the only motel in Mercy. She had also booked Alex onto a flight to a town near Mercy. She then called Alex and gave him all the details.

Alex was ready to leave and left shortly after hearing from Brenda. He drove to the airport and left his car there to be available when he returned. He settled back into his airplane seat and opened the file Brenda had put together on Mariam. Brenda had been very thorough, as always. She even had a picture of Mariam from the school yearbook, where she was a teacher. She looked very different in this picture. The one Darrin had shown him was much more relaxed, but she looked happier in the school picture.

Alex studied the picture. He didn't know what it was, but for some reason, he was drawn to the image in the picture. Ever since he had looked at the picture

Darrin had shown him, he had known he had to find her and protect her. Alex started reading her file, but every few minutes, he would look back at the picture. He couldn't help himself.

Andrew reached Mercy before Alex. He checked in and went to his room. After stowing his clothes, he went out to look around and find a place to eat. As he passed the bookstore, he saw a nice-looking young lady at the door saying goodbye to a group of children. There was an older lady with her, and they were passing out bags of cookies.

"Goodbye, Miss Janice, thanks for reading for us," said a small girl.

"Goodbye, Sara, I am glad you enjoyed the reading. I'll see you soon," answered the young lady.

Andrew looked at her more closely. Mariam looked up and saw him looking at her. He smiled at her and went on to the café next door. Mariam stared after him for a minute before she waved the rest of the children goodbye. She glanced one last time at the café next door, and then she shrugged and went back into the bookstore to straighten up and get ready to go out with Charles.

"The children loved getting the cookies," Mariam said to Darci.

"It was fun to give them a treat," said Darci.

"Did you notice the man going into the café when the children were leaving?" asked Mariam.

"Yes, I saw him," said Darci.

"Did you know him?" asked Mariam.

"No, he was a stranger," said Darci. "Why, did your guardian angel say anything?"

"No, she is still being silent. Maybe I am jumping

at shadows," said Mariam. She turned back to cleaning.

"Charles asked me to go out for a meal," said Mariam, looking at Darci to see if she objected.

Darci smiled. "It is about time. I was getting disappointed in my grandson. A pretty young lady moves to town and he doesn't try to date her," said Darci with a laugh.

"He said he didn't want to rush me," said Mariam with a smile.

"If he moved any slower, he would be crawling," retorted Darci.

Mariam laughed. "It's just a meal," she said.

"It's a first step," declared Darci.

"I take it you approve," said Mariam.

"Charles is a fine young man, and you are the nicest young lady I have met in a long time. I definitely approve. I hope you have a good time," said Darci.

"Thanks," said Mariam. "I had better go and get ready. I'll see you in the morning."

"Good night," said Darci as Mariam went to her room. Darci smiled with satisfaction as she locked the store and left for the night. Not long after, a knock came at Mariam's door.

Mariam smiled at Charles and said hello. "Where are we going to eat?" she asked.

"I thought we could go for a drive and eat at a place I know out of town. You eat in the cafés here in town all the time. I thought you might like a different type of food," said Charles.

"That sounds like a good idea," said Mariam. "I would love to see a little more of the places around here."

Charles guided her to his car and helped her in. She fastened her seat belt as he went to the driver's side and took his seat.

Charles looked at her and smiled as they started out. He was happy he had finally asked her out.

She smiled back at him. It was nice to get out and not have to stay in her room all the time. Surely, she would be safe with Charles. He was the law and Darci's grandson. She settled back to enjoy the ride.

While Mariam and Charles were enjoying getting out of town, Alex was arriving in town. He checked into his motel room and called Andrew. He decided to join Andrew at the café for a meal.

Andrew smiled as Alex joined him at his table. After Alex had ordered, he passed the folder on Mariam over for Andrew.

Andrew opened the folder and saw the picture of Mariam on the first page. He looked at it closely.

"This is the young woman from the bookstore," he said.

"You have seen her?" asked Alex.

"Yes, as I was getting here, I saw her talking to a bunch of children. There was an older woman with her, and they were telling the children goodbye. After the children were gone, the girl and the woman went back inside and locked up. The older woman left, but the girl in the picture stayed. I think she is living in the back of the store," said Andrew.

"Is she still there?" asked Alex.

"No, a man in a uniform came by, and she left with him. It looked like they were going on a date," said Andrew.

Alex looked thoughtful. He did not like hearing

about Mariam dating someone, but he was glad she was alright. Alex looked up and smiled at Andrew.

"You have saved us a lot of the time we would have had to spend looking for Mariam. Did you see anyone else interested or watching her?" asked Alex.

"No, there was no one else around. There have been a lot of people coming and going, but they did not pay any special attention to Mariam," said Andrew.

Alex nodded. "Good, we are ahead of them," said Alex.

The two of them finished eating and took a stroll around town to get a feel for their surroundings. Everyone they passed smiled and nodded hello. It seemed to be a friendly town.

While Alex and Andrew were getting to know Mercy, Mariam and Charles were being seated in the dining room of the country restaurant outside of Mercy.

Mariam looked around with appreciation. It was a nice place with a homey atmosphere. She smiled at Charles.

"Are there any more jewels like this hiding around Mercy?" she asked.

"A few," agreed Charles with a smile. "I'll have to take you out again to show you around."

"I would like that," said Mariam with a smile.

Charles smiled with satisfaction, and they both looked at the menus to see what they wanted to order.

Charles smiled at the waitress waiting for their order. "What's good tonight, Kami?"

"The roast and mashed potatoes are smelling mighty good in the kitchen right now," she replied with a grin.

Charles closed his menu. "I'll have the roast and potatoes," he said.

Mariam closed her menu. "Make that two," she said.

The waitress wrote down their orders. "Is tea alright?" she asked.

Both Mariam and Charles agreed to tea, and she left to turn in their order.

Mariam sat up straight and looked around. She didn't see anyone suspicious.

Charles was looking at her curiously. "Is anything wrong?" asked Charles.

Mariam shook her head. "No, I was just startled when my guardian angel talked to me. She has been so quiet lately; I was getting used to the peace."

"What did she say?" asked Charles.

"She said, 'He is coming,'" said Mariam.

"She didn't warn of danger?" asked Charles.

Mariam shook her head. "She just said he is coming. It was as if she thought it was a good thing," said Mariam.

"How do you know it's an angel?" asked Charles.

"Because she told me she was my guardian angel," replied Mariam.

"She told you," said Charles.

Mariam nodded. "When I was young, I asked and she said that, as my guardian angel, she was sent to watch over me and keep me safe." Mariam looked down and blinked away tears. "I wish her help had extended to my family," said Mariam.

Charles reached over and squeezed her hand. "They may have had their own guardian angels, but they didn't listen to them like you did. They can't help us if we don't hear them," said Charles.

Mariam looked thoughtful. They sat back out of the way as Kami brought their food and sat it down in front of them.

"Oh, it smells so good," said Mariam.

"It tastes as good as it smells," said Kami. "I'll be right back with your tea."

They did not wait for the tea. They both took up their forks and started eating, savoring every bite.

The tea was welcome when it arrived. Kami smiled and told them to let her know if they needed anything. They both nodded agreement and continued enjoying their food.

CHAPTER 5

Charles drove Mariam back to the bookstore after they finished eating.

"Thank you for a very good meal and enjoyable company," said Mariam.

"I meant what I said. I am going to show you around," said Charles.

Mariam smiled. "I look forward to seeing more of Mercy," said Mariam. "This town spoke to me the first time I saw it. It made me feel like I had come home."

"I'm glad," said Charles.

After opening her car door, he walked with her to the door of the bookstore. Mariam unlocked the door of the bookstore and turned and smiled at Charles.

Charles leaned forward and lightly kissed her. Mariam looked up at Charles solemnly.

Charles looked at her inquiringly. "What's wrong?" he asked.

"I don't know," answered Mariam. "It felt wrong for us to be kissing. It was almost like kissing my brother. My guardian angel said no."

Charles stared at her. "Your guardian angel told you not to kiss me," said Charles incredulously.

Mariam nodded. "She has never done that before," she said.

"I wish she had not picked me to start on," said Charles.

Mariam laughed. Charles stared at her. "I'm sorry. I don't mean to laugh at you, but you look so much like a youngster who has been told they can't have another cookie," said Mariam.

Charles shook his head and grinned at her. "I have never had a guardian angel tell me no before," he said. "It will take some getting used to. You had better get inside so I can be sure you are locked up before I leave."

"Okay," said Mariam. She turned and entered the store. Inside, she turned back to Charles. "Thanks for taking me out."

"You are welcome," said Charles with a smile. "I'm still going to show you around. Maybe your guardian angel will change her mind about me."

"Good night, Charles," said Mariam as she closed and locked the door. She waved at him and headed for her room.

Charles watched until she entered her room then turned and left.

Neither of them noticed Andrew hiding across the street watching them. He was behind a tree. Alex had asked him to keep an eye out for strangers. Andrew smiled and shook his head. He didn't know how he was supposed to do it. Everyone in town was a stranger to him. He sighed; at least he could stop the witch hunters from harming Mariam. After Mariam's light went out and he decided she was in for the night, he headed back to the motel to report to Alex.

Alex opened the door to Andrew's quiet knock. He stood back and motioned him to come inside. After Andrew came in, Alex glanced around before shutting the door. Satisfied no one was paying any attention to them; he shut the door and turned to Andrew.

Andrew looked at Alex and smiled. "Miss Semp is back in her room and in for the night. There was no one watching her, but me," he said.

"Good," said Alex. "You have to remember to call her Miss Janice."

"I'll remember," said Andrew. "How did a pretty girl like her draw the attention of those crackpot witch hunters?"

"She hears the voice of her guardian angel. She warns her of danger," said Alex.

"Cool," said Andrew. "Something like that could come in very handy in our line of work."

"Yes, it could," agreed Alex. "Why don't you try to get some sleep? We will take up guard duty in the morning, and I will introduce myself to Mariam. She should know we are here to protect her. I don't want her to mistake us for witch hunters."

"Okay," said Andrew. "I'll see you in the morning."

Andrew left, and Alex decided to take a stroll by the bookstore. He wanted to feel close to Mariam.

Mariam changed and prepared for bed. She started to lie down, but for some reason, she couldn't settle. She went out into the bookstore and walked around. Everything looked okay, but something was nagging at her.

Mariam started to turn and go back to her room when she looked out the window and saw a man standing looking at the bookstore. Mariam drew back where she would not be seen and stared at the man.

"He is here," said the voice of her guardian angel.

"Who is here?" asked Mariam.

"Your destiny," said the voice.

"What?" exclaimed Mariam! "How can he be my destiny? I don't know him."

"You will," replied her guardian angel. "Isn't he yummy?"

"Are you looking for someone for me or you?" asked Mariam.

"He is for you, but I can appreciate the scenery," answered her guardian angel.

Mariam looked at the stranger again. Her guardian angel was right. He did look yummy. She could only stand and stare at him.

Alex sighed and glanced around. He felt as if he was being watched, but there was no one in sight, after one last look at the bookstore, he turned and made his way back to the motel.

Mariam stood in the shadows and watched him leave.

"Don't worry," said her guardian angel. "He will be back. He is your destiny."

Mariam did not say anything. She made her way back to her room and lay down to sleep. She lay there thinking about the yummy guy from outside. She finally drifted off. She felt safer than she had in a long time.

Alex returned to his motel room and tried to sleep. He lay awake thinking about His reaction to the picture of Mariam. He would be glad when they had their first meeting over with and he could get over this feeling. He could only wait and see and hope for the best.

~

The next morning Mariam was very quiet as she went about her work. Darci glanced at her several times, but Mariam was preoccupied and did not notice. Finally, when Mariam came by the desk with an armload of books to shelve, Darci followed her over to the shelf.

"Did you and Charles have a good time last night?" Darci asked.

"Yes, it was a lovely restaurant. I loved being able to see more of Mercy," said Mariam.

"What is wrong? Did something happen?" asked Darci.

Mariam glanced at Darci. "Charles kissed me when he brought me home," said Mariam.

Darci stared at her and waited for her to continue.

"Nothing is going to happen between Charles and me. It felt like I was kissing my brother, and my guardian angel told me Charles wasn't for me. She said my destiny is here, but Charles isn't it," replied Mariam.

"I see," said Darci. "I'm sorry. I hoped you and Charles would get together. Did your guardian angel give you any idea who is your destiny?"

Mariam nodded. "I don't know who he is, but I got a glimpse of him last night."

"What did he look like?" asked Darci.

Mariam was staring at the door of the bookstore where Alex was entering.

"Like the man coming in the door," said Mariam quietly.

Darci turned and looked toward the door, startled. She stared at Alex.

"He's nice-looking," she said after giving Alex the once over.

"Yes," agreed Mariam.

Alex looked around and spotted Mariam and Darci at the bookshelves. He started over to join them. Mariam turned and put the remaining books on the shelf.

"Can I help you," asked Darci with a smile.

Alex smiled back at her. "I came in to introduce myself to Miss Janice. My name is Alex Avorn," he said, holding out his hand.

Mariam automatically took his hand. "You are Mark's brother," she said.

"Yes," Alex agreed. "Your brother asked me to look out for you."

"How did you find me?" asked Mariam.

"There was a request for information about you from the sheriff's office here," said Alex.

Mariam glanced at Darci. Darci looked startled. "Charles must have put your name through the system when you first came," she said.

"I need to go. I don't want to put you in danger. If Mr. Avorn can find me, the witch hunters could be right behind him," said Mariam.

"You are not going anywhere," said Darci. "We need to stop those witch hunters in their tracks. We can get Charles in and find a way to stop them once and for all."

"I agree," said Alex. He had been glancing back and forth between Darci and Mariam as they talked.

"I have one of my men with me, and I can bring in more. If we don't stop them now, you will be running and hiding from them for the rest of your life."

Mariam glanced down at her hand that was still being held by Alex. She gently withdrew it from his hand. Alex reluctantly let her pull away. They all turned and looked at the door as Andrew came in.

Mariam looked at Andrew and then glanced at Alex.

Alex smiled at her. "It is alright, this is my associate, Andrew Salto."

"It's nice to meet you, Miss Janice," said Andrew.

"Thank you. This is Darci Holt. She is the bookstore owner," said Mariam, motioning at Darci.

Both Alex and Andrew nodded and said hello to Darci.

"What do we do now?" asked Mariam.

"Now, I am going to call Charles and get him over here to meet Mr. Avorn and Mr. Salto," said Darci.

Alex nodded. "He needs to be here," agreed Alex.

Darci went over to the counter to call Charles, and Andrew smiled at Mariam.

"Do you really hear a voice warning you of danger?" he asked.

Mariam glanced sharply at Alex, and then looked at Andrew.

"Yes, it's my guardian angel. It doesn't make me a witch," said Mariam.

Andrew held up his hands in surrender. "I didn't think it did. I was just telling Alex, last night, I think it would be cool to have a voice warn of danger. It could come in handy in our line of work," he said with a smile.

Mariam laughed. "I can see where it might," she said.

Alex was listening and trying not to stare too much at Mariam. Mariam was having a hard time keeping her eyes from straying back to Alex.

Darci came back over. "Charles said he will be right over," she said.

"Did your guardian angel warn you of danger about us?" asked Alex looking back at Mariam.

"No, I think she was smitten by you," grinned Mariam.

"Me! When did she see me?" asked Alex.

"Last night outside the bookstore," said Mariam.

"Busted," said Andrew with a laugh.

"I was just looking around," said Alex.

They all turned and looked as Charles came in the bookstore.

Charles joined them at the bookshelves.

"Charles," said Darci. "This is Mr. Avorn and Mr. Salto. They were hired by Mariam's brother to find her and keep her safe. They found her through the inquiry you made about her."

Charles looked startled. He glanced at Mariam and flushed slightly.

"It was when you first came. I had to protect Grandma," said Charles.

"I know," said Mariam gently. "It is alright. I understand."

Alex looked at her as she comforted Charles.

"Who is your grandmother?" asked Alex.

"Darci," said Mariam. "She has been very good to me, even gave me a place to live. Charles had every right to be sure Darci was not in danger."

Alex took her hand. "I'm not saying he didn't. I'm

just trying to understand what is going on and figure out a way to stop the witch hunters before they hurt or kill anyone else," said Alex.

Everyone was watching Alex and Mariam. Mariam flushed and looked embarrassed.

"I'm sorry," said Mariam. "I need to stop jumping to conclusions."

Charles was watching Mariam's interaction with Alex. He sighed. He understood what Mariam was trying to tell him last night. He and Mariam would make great friends, but there was no spark between them like there was between her and Alex. It was easy to see they were drawn to each other. They might be fighting it, but it was there.

Alex squeezed her hand. "You don't need to be sorry. We need to sit down together and decide what we are going to do," said Alex.

"The first thing I'm going to do is hire a guard for the bookstore," said Charles. "Kenny is a retired police officer. He is a friend, and I trust him."

"No," said Darci. "I will not have Kenny Moore following me around. You know he has been after me ever since your granddad died. I have been able to avoid him so far. You are not going to put him in my store where I can't get away from him."

Darci stood with her hands on her hips, glaring at Charles. Mariam, Alex, and Andrew watched them with grins on their faces.

"Grandma, would you have Mariam in danger just because you can't handle Kenny," said Charles.

Darci looked at Mariam apologetically. "I didn't say I couldn't handle Kenny. I said I didn't want to, but I don't want Mariam in danger, and Kenny is a good officer, even if he is retired. You can hire him," said Darci.

"Thanks, Darci," said Mariam.

Darci smiled at her. "I would never forgive myself if anything happened to you because of me."

Charles hugged his grandma and then turned back to the group.

"I'm going to bring, Sammy, my German Shepherd over to watch at night. If anyone comes around, Sammy will sound the alarm," said Charles.

Everyone was nodding agreement.

"I will have Andrew and a couple of my other guys arrange a schedule to keep watch on the outside," said Alex.

"I really want to catch these guys. They have been terrorizing people long enough," said Charles.

"They are dangerous," whispered Mariam. "They thought nothing of burning my family."

"We will get them," promised Alex. He pulled Mariam close, and she hid her face in his chest.

Andrew grinned. He was seeing a different side of Alex. He couldn't blame him about Mariam. She was a knockout.

Charles took out his phone and went over to the desk to call Kenny. Kenny was delighted to help. He was tired of retirement, and he really was in love with Darci. He had been for years. He had never said anything because she was happily married, but after her husband died, he began going after his dream. The only problem was Darci. She avoided him whenever she saw him coming. Maybe he could get her to stand still long enough to see how good the two of them would be together if they were around each other more.

Charles hung up and returned to the others. "Kenny will start in the morning." He gave Darci a stern look. "You don't give Kenny a hard time. He is doing me a favor."

"I'll be an angel," said Darci looking innocent.

Charles gave her a skeptical look but didn't say anything.

"Are you two staying at the motel?" asked Charles.

"Yes, we are. There was nowhere else to stay," said Alex.

"I have a large house. You can stay with me. It will draw too much attention to you if you stay on at the motel," said Charles.

"Won't we draw attention staying with you?" asked Andrew.

"Not if you are my cousin Andrew and his friend. Everyone will expect you to stay with me, and I really do have a Cousin Andrew. He has never been here, so no one will know what he looks like," said Charles.

"Okay," said Andrew. "It's a pleasure to meet you, Cousin Charles."

"I need to go and get Sammy. If you come with me, you can check out of the motel, and it will give us a chance for people to see us together," said Charles.

Andrew looked at Alex, who nodded okay with the plan, then he followed Charles out.

When they were gone, Alex looked at Mariam. He still held her in his arms. He sighed. His arms were going to feel awfully empty when he had to release her.

Mariam pulled back and looked at Darci. The bell over the door rang as someone entered.

Darci and Mariam both smiled as Lana entered with Sara.

"Hi, Miss Janice," said Sara. "I talked Mom into coming back for the book I was reading yesterday."

Mariam smiled at Lana. "I will help you find it, Sara," said Mariam. She took Sara's hand and led her toward the children's books.

Alex sighed and watched her go. He missed her touch. He looked up and saw Sara's mom staring at him. He gave her a nod but did not encourage conversation. He followed Mariam with his eyes.

Darci smiled as she watched Lana's pouting face. She was too used to people pandering to her. It would do her good to see someone else be the center of attention for a change.

Mariam and Sara came back with the book. Darci rang up the sale, and Lana and Sara left with Lana giving Alex one last look. He didn't even see it. He only saw Mariam.

$\mathcal{M}$ariam walked over to Alex after Lana and Sara left. She smiled at him, and he smiled back at her and reached for her hand.

"What happens now?" she asked.

"We make sure you and Darci are safe, and then we set a trap for the witch hunters," said Alex.

Darci came over to join them. "Are we going to try and lure them to town so we can catch them?" asked Darci.

Mariam shivered. "It sounds dangerous."

"I promise you will be protected," said Alex.

"What are we going to do with them when we catch them? If they go to jail, they won't stay long, and then they will be a threat again," said Darci.

"I have something else in mind for them," said Alex.

"You are not planning on doing anything illegal, are you?" asked Mariam.

Alex smiled and squeezed her hand. "No, I have someone in my employ that can reprogram them," said Alex.

"Reprogram, what does that mean?" asked Darci.

"It means he can make the witch hunter forget all about hunting witches. He can make the person swear there is no such thing as witches. He will believe the people trying to make him believe in witches are a bunch of crackpots," said Alex grinning at the ladies.

"He can change a person's whole outlook," said Darci.

Alex nodded. "Yes, he can. We just have to catch them and hand them over to him," agreed Alex.

Darci rubbed her hands together. "What are we waiting for? Let's catch us some witch hunters. I want to see your friend in action," said Darci.

Mariam and Alex laughed at her enthusiasm.

"Is he a witch?" asked Mariam.

"No, he has a guardian angel just like all of us. He has just worked with his guardian angel to get it to talk to other guardian angels. They help each other with their charges. Most people don't know they have a guardian angel, so they don't guard against them. The guardian angel can then go into their mind and convince them to the right way of thinking," said Alex.

"How do we know the witch hunter won't revert back later on?" asked Mariam.

She and Darci were looking at Alex, and Darci nodded in agreement with Mariam.

"We keep an eye on his subjects, and so far, no one has changed back," said Alex.

Mariam looked at Darci. "It sounds wonderful," she said.

Darci nodded. "We need to get Charles in and tell him about this. I know he has been worried about what would happen when we caught the witch hunters," said Darci. "We could close down some prisons if we could turn your friend loose in there."

"He's only one man," said Alex. "He can only do so much. If we could train some others to do the same thing, we could get rid of crime."

Darci nodded with a shrug and walked away, leaving them alone.

Mariam gazed up at Alex with sparkling eyes. He looked back at her and sighed. "What is wrong?" she asked softly.

Alex glanced at Darci. She was at the cash register helping a customer.

"I am falling more in love with you by the second," he said softly.

"I am glad," said Mariam smiling. "My guardian angel said you were my destiny. I only know I have been drawn to you since I saw you outside the bookstore last night."

"Can you take a break and go next door for coffee?" asked Alex.

"Let me tell Darci where we are going," said Mariam. She tried to release his hand, but he held on and went to the cash register with her, still holding her hand.

Darci waved them on when they told her where they were going. As they were going out the door, an older man was coming in. He smiled at them, and they smiled back.

Before the door closed, they heard Darci say, "Kenny Moore, you didn't waste any time getting here."

"Charles asked me to come right over, Darci," said Kenny.

The door closed and Mariam and Alex went on

into the café next door and sat at a table. They held hands and waited quietly for the waitress to bring them coffee.

Mariam smiled at Alex.

"I can't believe I have found you," said Alex smiling at her lovingly.

"I can't believe it either," said Mariam. "Especially after all of the precautions I took not to be found."

"After I found out about the truck route coming to Mercy, and the inquiry from here, it all fell into place," said Alex.

"How did you know about the truck? The truck driver didn't know I hitched a ride with him," said Mariam.

"How did you manage to get a ride without the truck driver knowing?" asked Alex.

"I hid behind the seat, on the floor, under a blanket, while he was in the truck stop. I fell asleep, and when I woke up, I was in Mercy," said Mariam. "I think my guardian angel wanted me here. She knew I would be safe here."

"You were very lucky," said Alex. "I am so glad you had your guardian angel looking out for you."

"Me, too," agreed Mariam. "You saw Darrin. How is he doing?"

"He is okay. He is very worried about you, but I am keeping in touch with him through Mark. He knows I found you, and I will keep you safe. He is going to be shipping out soon, so knowing I am looking after you will make it easier for him."

"Will you pass a message to him and let him know I am sorry I couldn't be at the funeral," said Mariam.

"He knew you would be there if you could. It is

one reason why he was so worried. When he gets back from overseas, you can have a private memorial service together for your family to say goodbye," said Alex.

"I would like that," said Mariam, looking at Alex with shinning, misty eyes.

Alex squeezed her hand. "I think Darrin will like it, too."

"I need to get back to work. I can't leave Darci alone to do my job," said Mariam. "I wonder how she is dealing with Kenny."

"I'm sure Darci can handle him," said Alex with a grin as he paid for the coffee they didn't drink and escorted Mariam back to the bookstore.

Kenny was standing just inside the door when they entered. Alex smiled at him and turned loose of Mariam's hand so he could greet Kenny.

"Hello, I'm Alex Avorn. I'm looking out for Mariam," said Alex, holding out his hand to Kenny.

Kenny shook his hand and looked at him closely. "You are Avorn Security," said Kenny.

Alex looked surprised. "You've heard of me?" he asked.

"I keep up with what's going on in law enforcement," said Kenny. "You have solved some major cases the last few years."

"I have a good team, and we have been lucky," said Alex.

"It will be a pleasure working with you," said Kenny. "Maybe we can clear out these witch hunters once and for all."

"I hope so," said Mariam.

Kenny looked at her and smiled. "You don't have anything to worry about. With me and Alex watching out for you and Darci, those witch hunters had better find a new profession."

"Thank you, Kenny," said Mariam.

Darci had been watching and listening, but not saying anything. She was glad to hear such good things about Alex. She knew Mariam was falling for him, and he was just as enthralled with her.

Darci had become very fond of Mariam. She wanted her to be happy. If she couldn't be for Charles, then maybe Alex would be the one to make her happy. If so, she was all for them getting together.

Mariam turned and left the men talking as she made her way over to Darci at the counter. "Are you okay?" asked Mariam.

Darci smiled. "I'm a tough old bird. I can handle a little disruption," she said. "We need to find something for them to do so they won't be underfoot all the time."

Mariam glanced at Kenny and Alex. "What?" she asked.

"Let's get them to move the table in the break room out to the front. We can put the coffee maker on the table and some chairs around it. They can watch everyone coming and going and take turns scouting around. Alex would be able to make phone calls, and best of all, they would be out of our way," concluded Darci.

"Okay," said Mariam. "I'll see what I can do."

Darci grinned as Mariam went over to Alex and Kenny.

Mariam smiled at the guys and looked at Alex. "Darci was wondering if you guys would help us do a little rearranging," she said.

Both of then smiled and nodded.

"What does she want rearranged?" asked Alex.

"She wants to bring a table from the break room out here and put it in the open space in front of the window. If we put chairs around it and the coffee maker on it, there should be a good view of the door so anyone coming or going would be seen," said Mariam.

"More than likely she just wants to keep us out of her way," remarked Kenny with a frown in Darci's direction. His frown was wasted because Darci wasn't looking. She was busy with bookwork and making sure not to make eye contact.

"Come on," said Alex to Kenny. "You know we can't refuse a lady."

Mariam led the way to the break room and pointed out a table to be moved. Alex picked it up and turned it sideways to get it through the door. Kenny picked up two chairs and followed him. Mariam took the coffee maker from the counter and carried it out front. She sat it in the center of the table and went back for disposable cups and a cord for the coffee maker. Alex carried out two more chairs.

After everything was arranged, Mariam stood back and looked at the finished setting.

"It looks good there. We should have had it there all of the time," she said, looking at Darci.

Darci came over and looked it over. "It fits there nicely," she agreed. "Now, you guys can sit and stay out of my hair."

"I told you she just wanted us out of her way," said Kenny.

He and Alex pulled out chairs and sat down. "We won't get in your way," said Alex. "We know you have a business to run."

"Thanks, Alex," said Darci. "Having two good-looking guys sitting in my window should draw a lot of the women in."

"She is using us," said Kenny.

Darci and Mariam left to work.

"Did she just call us good looking?" asked Kenny softly to Alex.

"Yes, she did," agreed Alex, smiling at Kenny. "You don't mind if I make some phone calls, do you? I need to check in at my office and get things moving."

"Go ahead, I'm going to see if I can find some sugar and cream for our coffee." Kenny headed for the break room.

"Hello, Brenda," said Alex. "Has there been any news?

"Everything has been quiet. It makes me nervous when everything is this quiet. I feel like all hell is about to break loose," said Brenda.

Alex laughed. "We will be fine. We can handle whatever is thrown our way. Are Trey and Lori finished with their case?"

"Yes, they are on their way back to base. Do you want me to redirect them?"

"Yes, have them come to Mercy. They can use my motel room. I'm going to be staying with the local deputy sheriff," said Alex.

"How did that happen?" asked Brenda.

"He thought it would be less suspicious if Andrew and I stayed with him. Since Lori and Trey are a couple, they can pass as tourists," said Alex.

"I'll call them and get them headed your way. You want me to give them an update on the case?" asked Brenda.

"Just tell them the basics. I'll fill them in when they get here," said Alex.

"Okay, I'll get right on it," said Brenda.

"Thanks, Brenda," said Alex as he hung up the phone and was rejoined by Kenny with a creamer a sugar bowl and a box of donuts.

Alex laughed. "You mopped up," he remarked.

"I figured if Darci wanted a donut she would have to come over and talk to me to get it," said Kenny.

Alex shook his head, still laughing. He was going to enjoy watching Kenny and Darci's courtship. He glanced at Mariam, who was busy with a customer. He was going to enjoy his courtship, too.

When her customer left, Mariam made her way over to Alex, she stopped behind him and put her hand on his shoulder. Mariam looked down at the table and grinned when she spotted the donuts.

"Darci will be after you about her donuts. She gets a fresh box delivered every morning. The teenager working in the donut shop drops them by on his way to class," said Mariam.

"She is welcome to come and help herself," said Kenny looking smug.

"Don't say you weren't warned," said Mariam. She gave Alex's shoulder one last squeeze and went back to work.

Alex grinned at Kenny as Kenny picked up a donut with a napkin and started eating it with Darci watching.

Darci frowned and looked away. When she had her head turned where Kenny could not see her face, she smiled to herself. She was enjoying playing games with Kenny. She couldn't let him know or she would never be able to get rid of him.

Darci frowned again. She was not so sure she wanted to get rid of Kenny. He made her feel alive again. She felt like she had been asleep since her husband's death. Now, she felt like she was waking up. She didn't know how she felt about that. Darci looked over at Kenny again. *Time will tell*, she thought.

CHAPTER 7

Charles and Andrew returned to the bookstore with Sammy. Charles looked surprised to see Alex and Kenny sitting at a table in front of the store while enjoying a donut. He made his way over and pulled out a chair and sat down. Sammy sat beside him and watched what everyone was doing. Charles handed him a doggie treat to eat while they were eating donuts. Andrew joined them and took the last chair.

"How did this come about?" asked Charles.

"It was Darci's idea," said Kenny. "She thinks she will keep me out of her way."

Charles grinned and reached for a donut. "At least you have the donuts. When I was here last week, she wouldn't let me have one," said Charles.

Andrew started to reach for one but pulled his hand back at Charles' words.

"Darci, is it okay for me to have a donut?" he called out.

Darci looked over at the table, startled. When she saw it was Andrew asking and Charles was already eating a donut, she walked over to the table.

She took the box of donuts and held them out to Andrew. "Here, Andrew, help yourself," she said to Andrew. She glared at the others. "At least Andrew was polite enough to ask," she said. She turned and petted Sammy on his head and then went back to work. Charles looked after his grandma sheepishly, but he finished the donut and reached for a cup of coffee.

Alex grinned as he continued to work on his smartphone. He was glad he could access the internet. He was able to get a lot done and make sure Mariam was safe at the same time.

"Did you get moved into Charles' house?" asked Alex.

"Yes, I gave up my room. I wasn't sure what you wanted to do about the rooms," said Andrew.

"It's okay. I am going to let Trey and Lori have mine. I don't have much unpacked. It won't take me long to repack," said Alex.

"Trey and Lori are coming? Did they finish their case?" asked Andrew.

"Yes," said Alex.

"Who are Trey and Lori?" asked Charles.

"Trey and Lori Loden. They are two of my best operatives, who are married to each other," said Alex.

"Trey's name is Wayne Reginald Loden III," said Andrew.

"Wow, I can see why they call him Trey," said Charles.

Alex gave Andrew a stern look. Andrew looked away sheepishly.

"I'm sorry, I didn't stop to think. Alex is always telling me to think before I talk," said Andrew.

"Does Trey not want people to know his name?" asked Charles.

"He tries to keep a low profile. His father stirs up a lot of publicity, and Trey tries to avoid being caught in the backlash," said Alex.

"Oh," said Charles. "His father is Reggie Loden, the movie star."

"Yes, I would appreciate it if you wouldn't mention it to Trey," said Alex.

"I won't say a word," promised Charles.

"Me either," agreed Kenny.

"I promise to keep my mouth shut from now on," said Andrew.

Alex glanced at Andrew and then turned to Charles. "Charles, I want you to go back to your office and do a search for any information on Mariam Semp. Just a simple request; it should catch the witch hunter's attention. When they get here, we can catch them and reprogram them so we can quit worrying about them," said Alex.

"Reprogram them? How do you do that?" asked Charles.

"We let Trey talk to their guardian angels. When he is through, they will swear there are no such things as witches and people who think there are witches are crazy and they should stay away from them," said Alex.

"Does it really work?" asked Charles.

"Every case we have worked on so far has worked like a charm," said Alex with a grin.

Charles looked at Alex with a big grin on his face. "It will be better than putting them in jail. I was worried about them in jail. I knew they wouldn't stay long, and then they would be out and after my grandma again."

"When we are through with them, there will be no need for jail. They will leave and stay away of their own free will," said Alex.

Charles stood up and prepared to go. He had a smile on his face. "I hope this works." He took Sammy with him as he went over and told Darci goodbye. She was a little stiff with him, but she let him kiss her cheek. He told Sammy to stay and watch after Darci. Sammy sat down next to Darci, and Sammy and Darci watched Charles as he left. Darci looked over at the table and caught Alex's eye. He nodded at her, and she relaxed a little. Darci absently petted Sammy on his head.

A customer came in, and Darci turned her attention to her. Alex went back to his phone, and Kenny got up and made the rounds checking for anything suspicious.

Alex looked at Andrew. "Look around outside and find a good spot to keep an eye on the bookstore, maybe from the park or a nearby roof. We don't want to make anyone suspicious, so be inconspicuous," said Alex.

"Okay." Andrew rose and taking another donut he headed outside.

Alex shook his head. Andrew was young, but he was learning. He would be a topnotch operative in a few years. He just needed training and experience.

Alex looked at his phone. He had an incoming call from Mark.

"Hello, Mark," said Alex. "Have you received orders to ship out yet?"

"Yes, we leave tomorrow. Is Mariam anywhere

close by? Darrin is here, and he really wanted to talk to her before we go," said Mark.

"Yes, hold on."

Alex took his phone and went to find Mariam. He found her in between the bookshelves. "Can we go to the break room? Darrin is on the phone, and he wants to speak with you."

Mariam led the way into her room instead of the break room. When they were inside with the door closed, she turned to Alex.

"Mark, put Darrin on," said Alex. He handed the phone to Mariam.

"Hello, Mariam, is it really you?" asked Darrin.

"Yes, it is really me. I am so sorry I couldn't be there for the funeral."

"I know. I just want you to be safe. We can have a memorial service when I get home. You stay close to Alex and let him take care of you," said Darrin.

"I will," promised Mariam. "When do you leave?"

"I leave tomorrow. I hate leaving while you are in danger," said Darrin.

"Alex will take care of me. You stay safe and come back safely," said Mariam.

"I'll do my best," said Darrin.

"Before you go, I want you to know, Alex and I are in love. My guardian angel says he is my destiny. So, you know we are going to take care of each other. I want to thank you for sending him to me," said Mariam.

"I'm happy for you. I love you, and I will write. I will let Mark enclose my letters with his to Alex. You can send me letters the same way to Mark," said Darrin.

"Okay, I love you too," said Mariam."

"Let me talk to Alex for a minute," said Darrin.

Mariam handed the phone to Alex. "He wants to speak to you."

"Hello, Darrin," said Alex.

"Take good care of my sister, Alex. Is she right? Are you two in love?" asked Darrin.

"Yes, I love her, and I will protect her with my life," said Alex.

"I'm happy for you both, and I will see you when I get back," said Darrin.

"You and Mark stay safe. Don't worry about us. I have everything under control," said Alex.

"Mark wants to say goodbye." Darrin handed the phone to Mark.

"Hi, Alex," said Mark. "I just wanted to say goodbye and stay safe."

"I will. You and Darrin stay safe and come back to us. Mariam is going to be a part of our family. That means Darrin will be a part of our family, too. I love you, little brother," said Alex.

"I love you, too. Bye, Alex," said Mark.

After the call ended, Mariam went into Alex's arms. They closed tightly around her. Alex kissed her gently.

Mariam pulled back slightly. "I have to get back to work."

"Okay," said Alex as he kissed her again.

Mariam snuggled closer to him and kissed him back.

They went out in the bookstore so Mariam could get back to work. Darci saw them come back, and she thought Mariam looked like she had been crying. Darci and Sammy went over to Mariam.

"Are you alright?" asked Darci, looking at Mariam.

"I'm fine. I just talked to my brother, Darrin. Alex's brother, Mark, called so we could talk before they ship out tomorrow," said Mariam with shiny eyes.

"I'm glad you managed to talk to him. I know you have been missing him," said Darci.

"I really wanted to hear his voice and let him know he didn't have to worry about me. He will be gone for a year, and I didn't want him worrying about what was going on with me," said Mariam. She held out her hand for Sammy to smell before petting him on his head.

"Why don't you take a lunch break now? It's almost lunchtime, and it is quiet. You need to take a breather before we have to deal with the witch hunters," said Darci.

Mariam glanced up at Alex. He nodded.

"I need to collect my things from the motel and take them over to Charles' house so Trey and Lori can have the room when they get here, then we can grab some lunch before you have to come back to work," said Alex.

Mariam nodded. "We'll see you after lunch," she told Darci. With one last pat for Sammy, she and Alex headed for the door.

Darci waved them on and went to help a customer.

Kenny came by a few minutes later.

"Do you know where Alex is?" he asked Darci.

"He and Mariam went to lunch," said Darci.

Kenny nodded and held out a hand to Sammy.

He then rubbed Sammy's head and stood back, watching as Darci waited on a customer.

The customer looked at Kenny curiously, wondering what he was doing hanging around the bookstore.

Darci finished with the customer and sent her on her way. She noticed how curious the lady had been. *Nosy people*, Darci thought.

When the customer was gone, Darci turned and looked at Kenny petting Sammy and frowned. Kenny smiled at her.

"Sammy is going to be spoiled," Darci said. "Don't you have anything to do besides standing looking at me?" she asked.

"I enjoy standing and looking at you," said Kenny with a grin. "It is a pleasure I don't get all of the time. I want to enjoy it while I can."

"Why me?" asked Darci.

Kenny looked serious. "I don't know why. All I know is I have been in love with you for years, and I must let you know how I feel before it is too late. I'm not getting any younger," said Kenny.

"You're not sick, are you?" asked Darci, looking at him sharply.

"No," said Kenny smiling gently. "I am fine, just aware of the passing years."

Darci shook her head. "You don't have anything to worry about. You are in the prime of life."

Another customer came into the door, and Kenny went over to the table to sit and enjoy watching Darci. He smiled widely. He was finally where he wanted to be, close to Darci. Sammy stayed close to Darci, also. Charles had given him his orders, and he was very obedient.

While Darci was taking care of her customer, she kept glancing over at Kenny. It was beginning to feel natural to have him around.

~

Meanwhile, Alex and Mariam had picked up what luggage he had left at the motel. Alex called Trey and given him the room number and address so he and Lori could use the room without having to go to the office and check in. He told him he would leave the key inside and the door unlocked.

"I will have to go to Charles' house later. I don't have a key to get in. I'll just leave my luggage in the car, and we can go to lunch," said Alex.

Mariam laughed. "Bad planning," said Mariam.

"I had other things on my mind," agreed Alex smiling at her.

"Do you want to go by the grocery store and pick up some sandwiches? We can eat in the park," suggested Mariam.

"I like your ideas," agreed Alex. "I love being out in the open. We can talk without everyone listening."

"It is a beautiful day outside," said Mariam.

They stopped at the grocery and shopped in the deli. They picked up chicken salad sandwiches with extra pickles. Alex threw in a couple of bags of chips, and Mariam enclosed a couple of sodas.

They took their goodies and walked into the park. They avoided the tables where people were sitting and headed for a secluded table off to one side. It was perfect. They could enjoy the outside and not worry about people.

"This is great," said Mariam, taking a bite of her sandwich.

"Yes," agreed Alex. "I will be glad when this case is completed and we can get on with our lives without worry."

Mariam looked down thoughtfully.

Alex glanced at her, and seeing her downcast face, gently lifted her chin with his hand.

"What's wrong?" he asked.

"I was thinking about when you are no longer worried about the witch hunters," said Mariam.

"Just because the case will be over doesn't mean we will be over," said Alex. "I have no intention of ever being without you in my life. I know we have a few things to work out, but we will work them out together. I love you. I am your destiny." Alex smiled. "And you are my destiny. We are going to be together," promised Alex.

He leaned forward and kissed Mariam. She kissed him back and then smiled mistily at him.

"I am so glad we found each other," said Mariam.

"Me, too," agreed Alex. "Eat your lunch. We don't want you to go back to work hungry."

Mariam obediently started eating her sandwich with bites in between of pickle.

"You know," said Mariam, "it's nice to know we have similar tastes in food."

Alex laughed. "It was meant to be."

They finished their food and disposed of their trash in a nearby trash can before heading back to the bookstore.

When Mariam and Alex arrived back at the bookstore, several children waited for Mariam to read to them. Mariam took them back and had them sit in a circle while she read them a story. They picked out books and went to be checked out by Darci. All of them had to pat Sammy on his head. He looked like he was smiling at them. He loved the attention, but he stayed close to Darci.

When Darci was asked about Sammy being there, she told them she was taking care of him for Charles.

After they left, Alex came over to the counter. "Darci, I think you should close the bookstore for a few days. You could put a sign in the window saying closed for inventory. I would hate for any of the children to be caught in the crossfire when the witch hunters show up," said Alex.

"You seem sure they are coming," said Darci.

"They will be here within a few days, just as soon as someone sees the information search Charles has sent out," said Alex.

Darci sighed. "I know you are right. I will make up a sign to put in the window."

While Darci was gone, Alex turned to Mariam. "We are going to make other arrangements for you. You cannot stay here by yourself at night."

"Where am I going to stay?" asked Mariam.

"With me," said Alex.

"I thought the whole idea was for me to draw them out so we could catch them," said Mariam.

"We will have to draw them out in the daytime or set a trap for them at night. I don't want you by yourself at night," said Alex. "We will have to make sure they know you are helping Darci with inventory. The rest of us will be here, but we will stay out of sight. They will try to find a way to get to you as soon as they can. They will be in a hurry to get to you because you got away from them before. They will not want to take a chance on losing you again."

"Before, they tried to run me down with a car, then they came after me with a gun. They did try to avoid being seen by anyone else," said Mariam.

"We will slip you out the back and have an armed guard stay in your room at night. We will also have someone hiding in the bookstore to help the person in your room. When the hunters see your light on at night after Darci leaves, they will think you are there. Hopefully, we will be able to trap them when they break in," said Alex.

"If they go to the café and ask questions, it will be easy for them to find out I am staying in the bookstore at night," said Mariam.

"It's one of the things about a small town. All you have to do is sit and listen, and you will find out everything to know about the town," said Alex.

"I like this small town," said Mariam. "The

people here have treated me really well when I needed help."

"I'm very grateful you found this place and these people when you needed them," said Alex, putting his arms around Mariam.

"I am, too," agreed Mariam.

Darci and Sammy returned with the sign. Kenny was trailing along behind them. Alex took the sign and went to tape it in the window. They wanted to be sure the people would be aware the bookstore would be closed for a few days.

Darci sighed. I will be glad when this is over," she said.

"I'm sorry I brought this trouble to the bookstore," said Mariam.

"It's not your fault. It was just a matter of time before the hunters came after me. They were just trying to build up the courage to face Charles. The older ones are more cautious, but the younger ones are cocky and think they are invincible. They would have had to test their luck. I am glad to finish it once and for all," said Darci.

"I don't know about getting it over with permanently," said Alex. "It all depends on if the ones coming after Mariam ask for help from the locals. Seeing them changed may make the young ones think twice about sticking their necks out."

"We will see," said Darci. "We may have to talk you and your group into staying around and clearing out the hunters around here."

Mariam looked at Alex and smiled. He was looking at Darci as if thinking about what she had said.

Alex's phone rang, and he went over to the table to take the call. He was back in a couple of minutes.

"Trey and Lori are here. They are getting settled in. As soon as they eat, they will be stopping by," said Alex.

"I am looking forward to meeting Trey," said Darci. "I want to see him in action."

Alex grinned. "It is something else to watch him in action."

They all looked toward the door as it opened and Charles entered.

"Good idea," said Charles, motioning to the sign in the window.

"It was Alex's idea," said Darci.

Mariam looked at Sammy. He was on alert when Charles entered, but he did not leave Darci's side.

Charles came over and patted his head. "Good boy," he said.

Mariam could have sworn Sammy preened under Charles' praise.

"How is everything going?" Charles asked Kenny.

"It has been quiet so far," said Kenny.

Charles glanced at Alex as if asking his view of the words Kenny had just offered.

"Trey and Lori have arrived. They are staying in my motel room. They will be by after they eat," said Alex. "I have my luggage in my car. I didn't have your address or a key, and I sent Andrew out to look around."

Mariam stiffened and looked at the window.

"They are here," she said.

All three guys turned and looked out the window.

"I don't see anyone," said Charles.

Mariam glanced at Charles. "My guardian angel

said they were here. She didn't say where they were, but they are sure to be close."

"They are probably out scouting around." said Alex. "They have no way of knowing you are in the bookstore until they talk to a few people. All they have to go on is Charles' inquiry."

"What should we do?" asked Kenny.

"Kenny, you and Charles sit at the table and drink some coffee. Act like nothing is wrong. Mariam, you and Darci make sure the back door is locked and then start working as if doing inventory," said Alex. "Let me know if your guardian angel says anything else."

"What are you going to do?" asked Mariam.

"I'm going to call Trey and hurry him and Lori along. They need to get here and look around before the hunters show up," said Alex.

Alex stepped behind a bookshelf to make his call. He could see the street, but no one could see him.

Mariam, Darci, and Sammy headed back to check the back door. Trey and Lori left the café next door and slowly strolled into the bookstore. Once inside the store, they nodded to Charles and Kenny and casually walked to the bookshelf where Alex was standing.

Lori grinned at Alex. "You just can't stay out of trouble, can you?" she said to Alex.

"It was just an excuse to get you two to come and join me," joked Alex.

Trey laughed. "We were getting bored anyway. Two days with nothing to do after our case was finished. We hardly knew what to do with all of the free time."

"Speak for yourself," said Lori. "I was getting ready for a nice long shopping spree."

"You saved my life, Alex. Thank you for saving me from the dreaded shopping spree," said Trey with a smile.

Mariam watched the couple's interaction, amazed at how easily they joked with each other.

Alex motioned for her and Darci to come over. He put his arm around Mariam and nodded at Darci. "Darci is the bookstore owner. Mariam is the one the hunters are after. Ladies, meet Trey and his better half, Lori," said Alex.

Lori laughed, and Trey looked hard at Alex. They both held out their hands to shake with Darci and Mariam. Sammy watched Lori shake hands with Darci, but when Trey started to shake hands, Sammy growled deep in his throat.

Darci looked at Sammy hard, but Trey froze and did not move.

"It's okay, Sammy, Trey is a friend. Hold your hand down so he can smell it," said Darci.

Trey slowly lowered his hand down and let Sammy sniff it.

Sammy sniffed Trey's hand and sat back as if giving permission for them to shake. Darci reached out and shook Trey's hand. Trey relaxed when Sammy sat and watched the handshake and didn't protest.

"I've shook hands with dignitaries with less ceremony," said Trey.

"Good boy," said Mariam, patting Sammy's head.

Lori reached over and patted Sammy's head, too. "He probably smelled Handsome on you," said Lori.

"Who is Handsome?" asked Darci.

"Trey's cat. She doesn't like me, so she mostly ignores me," said Lori.

Alex had motioned for Charles and Kenny to join them, and he took the guys to show Trey around. He wanted to keep them away from the window so no one could see how many people were in the bookstore.

Lori looked at Mariam. How long have the witch hunters been after you?" she asked

"It seems like forever, but it has only been almost two weeks since they burned my home and killed my parents and brother. If I had not had car trouble, they would have got me, too," said Mariam.

"I'm sorry about your family," said Lori. She hugged Mariam. "Don't you worry, we are here for you, and Alex never leaves a job until he wins, and I think you are more than just a job to him. I have never seen the look in Alex's eyes as he has when he looks at you."

Mariam flushed slightly. "I love him, and Alex says he loves me, too," she said.

"If Alex says it, you can believe it. He is the most honest man I know," said Lori. "If it wasn't for Alex, I wouldn't be with the love of my life. He helped Trey and I realize we were meant for each other."

The guys came back, and Trey casually draped an arm around Lori.

Alex, equally casual, put an arm around Mariam and pulled her close to his side.

"Trey thinks if we can trap the hunters in the store, we can administer a light sedative and take them one at a time to the back room and reprogram them," said Alex.

"We make them walk back to the room and then give them the sedative. I'm not lugging around any heavy hunters," said Trey.

Alex laughed. "I told you it wouldn't happen again."

Everyone looked at him curiously except Lori, who hid a smile.

"Things didn't go quite as planned with the last hunters," said Alex. "One of the hunters was giving us a problem, and Lori slapped him with the sedative. We had to carry him to a place to work on him. He weighed about 360 pounds. It took three of us to move him, and Trey swore he was carrying the heaviest part."

"What part was he carrying?" asked Darci.

"He was in the middle," said Lori. "Andrew was carrying his feet, and Alex had his head."

Darci looked at Trey and shook her head.

Trey flushed. "You would have to see him to understand," he said.

"Trey got his revenge," said Lori. "While he was talking to the guy, he told him he needed to lose down to 200 pounds or he would have a heart attack. The first thing he did when he woke up was tell his buddies he was on a diet and he was going to join a gym." They all laughed.

"It worked," said Trey. "When we checked on him to be sure our programming worked, he was already signed into a gym. He was on a strict diet and had already lost at least 50 pounds."

"Wow," said Mariam. "You could make a mint helping people with no willpower."

"I would be bored silly in that type of crowd. Working for Alex suits Lori and me. We get to work together, and it's never boring," said Trey.

"I'm very glad to have you both on my team," said Alex.

"Lori and I have been here long enough. We don't want anyone to get suspicious. Why don't we get us a book and head back to the motel? When we come back, I'll call and you can let us in the back door," said Trey.

Lori picked out a book, and she and Darci went to check it out. Terry joined her, and they strolled out the door together, holding hands.

Alex called Andrew and asked him if he had seen anything suspicious.

He said he had seen a car drive by slowly earlier. There were two men in the car, and they had not stopped anywhere. Alex told him to take a break and get something to eat so he could go back on watch later.

"Charles, why don't you send Darci home. She can take Sammy with her, and Kenny can go along to keep watch?" asked Alex.

"It's not long until closing time," said Charles to Darci. "Everyone will think you are closing early to get ready for inventory tomorrow."

"Okay," said Darci. "If you catch the hunters, you send for me and Kenny. I want to watch Trey in action."

"I will do my best," said Charles. "I don't know what is going to happen. I'll send for you if I can."

"What are my orders?" asked Mariam.

Alex looked at her inquiringly.

"You have been arranging everyone else, I was just wondering when you would get around to me," said Mariam.

Charles hid a smile as Alex looked lost for a reply.

Alex reached for Mariam and pulled her close.

"I don't want to let you out of my sight," he said with a sigh.

Mariam put her arms around him and snuggled close. "It would be good for me to stay here with you. My guardian angel will let me know when they come. It could help to have some advance warning," she said.

Alex looked thoughtful. "Do you know how to shoot a gun?"

"Yes," said Mariam. "Dad taught me and Darrin."

"You wouldn't happen to know how to give a shot would you?" asked Alex.

"Yes, I had to take a class in first aid before I could take the job of being a kindergarten teacher," said Mariam.

Alex smiled. "You can stay, but if I tell you to hide, you don't stop to ask questions, you hide," said Alex.

"I promise," said Mariam, smiling up at him.

Charles' phone rang. He listened for a minute, then said thanks and hung up. "Kenny said they are at his house. He thought it would be safer than Darci's. He said he checked it out, and they are settled in. Even Sammy is relaxing," said Charles with a smile.

CHAPTER 9

*A*lex's phone rang. He answered and then went to let Trey and Lori in the back door.

"Look who we found waiting for us at the motel," said Trey as he entered. He was followed by Lori and two more large, tough-looking guys.

Alex grinned and shook hands with two more of his agents.

"Glad you guys managed to get here before the action," said Alex.

"We are, too. You usually start without us," said Sal, grinning.

"Mariam, Charles, these are two of my agents. The big ugly one is Micky, and the bigger ugly one is Sal," said Alex.

"Guys, this is my lady, Mariam, and Deputy Sheriff Charles Holt," said Alex.

The guys nodded to Mariam and Charles.

"Pleased to meet you, Ma'am," said Micky.

"It's nice to meet you both," said Mariam with a smile.

"Don't let the boss fool you," said Sal. "He knows

we are better looking than him. He has to pretend otherwise to keep us from getting wise to his tricks."

"What kind of tricks?" asked Mariam with a grin.

"He doesn't think we can get any work done if we are distracted by the ladies," said Micky. "So, he sends us on jobs where the ladies are all married or too young for us. Then he tells us he didn't want to expose our ugly mugs to sensitive young ladies. We got him back, though. We told some young ladies we knew that he was very lonesome and could use some company. He couldn't go into work for a week without being mobbed by the young ladies. Brenda finally got rid of them by telling them that Alex was going to be out of the country working for a year."

Mariam and Charles laughed.

"I couldn't get any work done without another young lady popping up," said Alex. "If these two weren't such good agents, I would have fired them."

"You know you would miss us, Boss," said Sal with a grin.

Alex's phone rang, interrupting their banter.

"Hello, Andrew," said Alex.

"While I was eating at the café on the other side of the park, the two men in the car came in. They met up with two locals and sat down to talk with them. They showed the locals a picture of Mariam. One of them shook his head. He didn't know her. The other told them she was working at the bookstore. They sat talking about how to get to her for a while. Then all four got up to leave. The locals said something about them meeting their boss while they were leaving," said Andrew.

"Where are you now?" asked Alex.

"I am back in the park watching the bookstore," said Andrew.

"Keep a watch. If they look like they are going to try to get into the bookstore, ring my phone. Let it ring once and hang up. If they are trying anything else, keep ringing until I answer. I'll have my phone on vibrate," said Alex.

"Okay," agreed Andrew.

Alex hung up the phone and turned to the others.

"The hunters are on the move. They met up with two local hunters and showed them a picture of Mariam. They are on their way to meet up with the local boss now," said Alex.

"What do you want us to do?" asked Trey.

"I want you to wait in Mariam's room. Make sure the light is on but cover the windows so they can't see in. Make sure your shadow isn't seen from outside. Lori and Mariam can wait in the break room. Charles, you and Sal can hide in the stock room. Micky, you can hide in Darci's office.

"All of you keep your phones on low vibrate so they won't ring at the wrong time. Make sure you can't be seen from outside. When they come in, we want to knock them out and tie them up so Trey can work on them one at a time."

"Where are you going to be," asked Lori.

"I'm going to circulate," said Alex.

He took out a small handgun from his pocket and handed it to Mariam. "Please try not to shoot me or my men," said Alex.

"I'll try not to," said Mariam, examining the gun.

"Yes, please try hard," said Sal. "I really don't like getting shot."

Mariam looked at him and grinned. "Aren't you in

the wrong profession if you don't like being shot at?" she asked.

Sal shook his head. "The way things are going around the country, it's the safest profession to be in. I am armed, and most of the time, I have backup," said Sal.

Mariam thought about what he said and nodded her agreement.

"Let's get settled," said Alex. "We don't know when they are going to pay us a visit."

Everyone scattered to get into place. Alex went with Mariam and Lori to check out the break room.

After Alex looked around the break room, he pulled Mariam close and kissed her. "Stay safe," he said.

"You, too," said Mariam.

Alex slipped back out into the bookstore and found a spot where he could keep an eye on the front window without being seen.

Mariam and Lori went to the table and sat in the chairs.

"We may as well be relaxed for now," said Mariam. "My guardian angel will let me know when the hunters are close."

Mariam looked at Lori. The natural light from the moon was shining in the window in the break room. The window was high up, and no one would be able to get in it or see in it, but it did shine in enough light so they could see each other.

"Do all of you have guardian angels?" asked Mariam softly.

Lori nodded. "We all have them, but we each have different abilities. It's like the guardian angels know what we need, and they supply it," said Lori.

"What's your ability?" asked Mariam.

Lori smiled. "I can sing someone to sleep," she said.

Mariam smiled. "It could come in handy when you have a child," she said.

Lori looked away. "What's wrong?" asked Mariam.

"I can't have children. I was in an auto accident with my parents when I was small. The doctors had to do several surgeries. They said I was too damaged, and I would not be able to have children," said Lori.

"I'm sorry," said Mariam. "Have you considered adoption?"

"Trey and I have talked about it. It's in the cards for when we settle down a bit," said Lori.

"I'm glad. I think you and Trey will make great parents," said Mariam.

"What about you and Alex?" asked Lori.

"Alex and I haven't had a chance to talk about anything yet. We have been busy trying to make sure I survive the witch hunters. I am sure we will get around to it. I love children. It's why I became a teacher," said Mariam.

Mariam stiffened. "They are coming," she said.

Lori went to the door and cracked it open so she could warn Alex about the hunters. After she told Alex, she hurried back in and took Mariam by the arm and led her over to the side of the refrigerator. They stood up against the wall so they wouldn't be seen if anyone opened the door.

The ladies heard sounds of a struggle, but they didn't hear any shots. They stayed where they were and didn't come out. When things got quiet, they started to come out, but they heard the door to the break room start to open.

Mariam looked around Lori and saw the moonlight shining off a gun. The face that followed the gun into the room was not known to her. When Lori started to move forward, the man with the gun swung in their direction. Mariam pushed Lori down and fired at the hand of the man. The man dropped the gun and held his hand as he dropped to the floor.

Mariam went over and held her gun on the man. Alex and Sal came busting through the door.

Alex looked scared. He took the gun from Mariam and held her close. Sal held a gun on the witch hunter.

The other guys came bursting into the room. Trey went over and helped Lori up and hugged her close.

"What happened?" asked Alex, drawing back slightly and looking at Mariam.

"The hunter was going to shoot me, but Mariam pushed me out of the way and shot him," said Lori.

"Thank you, Mariam," said Trey. He hugged Lori closer.

"Mariam looked at Lori. "My guardian angel told me to protect the baby," said Mariam.

"What baby?" asked Lori.

"Your baby," said Mariam.

"I can't be pregnant. I can't have children," said Lori.

"My guardian angel said you were having a little girl, and I trust her over any doctor," said Mariam.

"We are going to be parents," said Trey grinning.

"You're sure?" asked Lori, looking at Mariam.

"I'm sure. I didn't hurt you pushing you down, did I?" asked Mariam.

"I'm fine," said Lori. "Thank you for saving me and my little girl." She pulled away from Trey and went over and hugged Mariam.

With misty eyes, both ladies looked at the guys. "Did we get them all?" asked Mariam.

"Yes, we did," said Sal with satisfaction.

"Now," said Alex. "We take them into the break room so Trey can work on them. Charles, call Kenny and tell him to bring Darci in through the back door. She wants to be here."

Charles stepped out to call Kenny. Sal and Micky bandaged the man who was shot and sat him in a chair to be Trey's first subject.

"Lori, will you and Mariam sit in these chairs and help?" asked Trey.

Lori and Mariam went over and sat in the other chairs. Trey took a rope and tied the man to the chair. Then Trey sat in a chair between Mariam and Lori and reached for a hand from each of them.

Trey sat back and closed his eyes. "Will our guardian angels come forth and talk to this man's guardian angel."

Trey nodded a couple of times. "Tell Neil there is no such thing as a witch. The people who pretend to believe in witches are nutcases. They want to get their thrills by fooling others into believing in witches. They want to fool others into doing stupid things so they can sit back and laugh at them."

Trey paused and listened for a minute.

"Tell Neil you are his guardian angel, and if the crackpot witch hunters knew about you, they would be after him, claiming he is a witch. Tell him we know he is not a witch because there is no such thing as a witch. Let our guardian angels band together and shower Neil with light.

"From now on, he is not going to even talk to the nutcase witch hunters. They are bad people. He is going to make some new friends and stay away from crackpots."

Trey paused again and listened. He smiled and let go of Lori and Mariam's hands. "It's done." He got up and untied Neil from the chair. Neil blinked at him as if he was awakening.

"You had better go see a doctor for your hand, Neil," said Trey. "You slammed the car door on it pretty hard. It might need stitches. Would you like someone to drive you?" asked Trey.

"No," said Neil. "Doc's office is just up the block. I'll walk over. I think the fresh air will do me good," said Neil.

"Okay," agreed Trey. "If you need anything, just let me know."

"I will, thanks," said Neil as Trey walked him out and let him out the front door and re-locked it behind him.

Alex smiled at the look of wonder on Mariam's face. Lori had witnessed Trey in action before, so she was not as in awe as Mariam.

"Bring in the next one," said Trey as he reentered the break room.

Darci and Kenny entered from the back, and Darci was seated and ready when they brought in the next young man and tied him to the chair.

Trey held Darci and Kenny's hands and used their guardian angels for this one. He wanted Lori to rest. He was still reeling from their news. He wanted to finish up so he and Lori could celebrate.

I'm going to be a dad, he thought, smiling. He glanced at Lori and found her looking at him with love and happiness in her eyes.

While Trey was dealing with the next hunter, Alex drew Mariam into her room and closed the door.

He held her close and kissed her. "When I heard the gunfire, my heart stood still. I was so scared." He squeezed her tight. After a few more kisses, Alex looked down at Mariam. "That was great shooting. It really could pass for getting slammed in a car door," said Alex.

"My dad was a great teacher. Darrin and I used to compete at the county fair. One of us almost always won the target practice shows. We had a bunch of ribbons, but they all were burned in the fire," said Mariam.

Alex hugged her again. "You have Darrin, and you have those memories. They can't take those away from you," said Alex.

Mariam pulled back slightly. "What happens now?" she asked.

"We wait a few days and see if anyone else shows up. If they don't, I will leave one of my guys here for a while to watch out for Darci. I have to get back to my office." Alex looked down at her. "Before you ask, you are coming with me. We are going to have to talk and decide a lot of things. I want to build a life with you. I love you."

"I love you, too," said Mariam. "I want to build a life with you, too. I don' really care where we build that life as long as we are together."

Alex pulled her close for another kiss. They pulled back when they heard a knock on the door.

Alex held her close to his side as he turned to open the door.

It was Micky. "Hey, Boss, Trey is on the last guy now. Sal and I were wondering if you want us to stick around or if we need to head on back."

"I want you and Sal to get a room at the motel. Put it on the office tab and get a good night's sleep before you go anywhere. Thanks for showing up when you did. It was great to have extra backup," said Alex.

"Sure. If you need us, just call," said Micky.

Micky went and found Sal, and they quietly left through the back door. They were gone for a few minutes before they were missed.

Trey sent the last hunter on his way as Darci watched with a big grin on her face. She was having the time of her life. Kenny watched over her with loving eyes and made sure she was okay. She turned and smiled at him. Things between them were much more relaxed and comfortable now.

Trey took Lori by the hand, and after saying goodnight, they also left out the back door.

"Where's Sammy?" asked Charles.

"We left him at Kenny's house," said Darcy. "I didn't want him to get hurt."

Charles shook his head. "I left him with you for protection," he said.

"You said they were caught when you called. I didn't need him then. Anyway, I had Kenny."

"Okay," said Charles. "Why don't you two go on home. I'll pick up Sammy in a couple of days. You stay with Kenny until I'm sure we have them all."

"Okay," said Darci. She and Kenny headed out the back door.

Charles shut the back door, and he put a police doorstop under the handle to be sure no one else could get in. Then he and Andrew led the way out the front with Mariam and Alex following. Mariam locked the front door, and she and Alex followed Charles and Andrew, in Alex's car, to Charles' house.

CHAPTER 10

They had just entered Charles' house when Alex's phone rang.

"Hello," said Alex.

"Alex, this is Trey. I picked up something from the first guy, the one who was shot. I should have told you, but I forgot about it while I was working on the other."

"What was it?" asked Alex.

"It was a name. Neil was thinking about someone who would be upset with him. He was thinking Mr. Talcove would be upset with him. He thought the boss wouldn't like this. He forgot all about it after the angels worked on him." said Trey. "I'm sorry I forgot. I had other things on my mind."

Alex grinned. "I bet you did. Congratulations to you and Lori."

"Thanks, we will see you tomorrow," said Trey.

"Good night," said Alex as he hung up the phone.

Andrew, Charles, and Mariam had been talking, waiting for Alex to finish his call. When he hung up, Mariam turned and looked at him.

"Is everything alright?" asked Mariam.

"Yes, they are fine. Trey forgot to tell me about getting the name of the local boss from Neil," said Alex.

"Who was it?" asked Charles.

"Somebody named Talcove," said Alex.

Charles stiffened and cursed.

"I take it you know him," said Alex.

"Yeah, I know him. He is our Mayor. He also happens to be married to my sister, Lana," said Charles.

"He's Sara's father?" asked Mariam.

"Yes," nodded Charles.

"Has he ever said anything about witches?" asked Alex.

"Not in my hearing. I did hear him call Darci an old witch one time, but I thought he was being sarcastic. I told him then he better not be disrespectful to my grandma again. He never said anything where I could hear him after then, but I don't know what he has said to Lana. She has not said anything to me," said Charles.

"When he finds out we broke up his gang, he may get nervous. You need to talk to Lana and advise her to be careful. If he is the boss, we are going to have to find a way to lure him into the bookstore and let Trey work on him," said Alex.

"Can we do this tomorrow?" asked Mariam. "It's been a long day."

"Sure," said Charles. "Andrew, you know where your room is. Could you show Alex and Mariam to the rooms across the hall from you? If you need anything, just let me know. If you are hungry, the kitchen is through the door behind you. You are welcome to help yourself. I'll say good night. I want to call the station and check in before I go to sleep."

They all said good night and headed upstairs. Andrew showed them their rooms and then went into his room, leaving Alex and Mariam standing in the hall in front of Mariam's room.

"I don't want to let you out of my sight," whispered Alex, drawing her close.

Mariam raised her face for his kiss and kissed him back. Alex finally drew back so they could breathe. He rested his forehead on hers and waited for their breathing to slow.

"Stay with me," whispered Alex. "We don't have to do anything. I just want to hold you close in my arms and know you are safe."

Mariam looked into his eyes and smiled. "I would like that," she said softly.

Alex opened his door and drew her inside and closed the door behind them.

"I don't have any clothes," said Mariam.

Alex laid his duffle bag on a chair. "I had Lori add your clothes to mine in my duffle bag. There was no way I was going to leave you in the room in the bookstore by yourself tonight," said Alex.

"Thank you," said Mariam. She reached up and gave him a quick kiss before opening the bag and pulling out her clothes. She took them over and laid them on the dresser. She didn't have a lot, just what she had bought at the resale store, but she did have a long tee-shirt to sleep in.

Mariam looked around and spotted the bathroom. She took her tee-shirt and went to change. She smiled at Alex, who was looking through his bag. Alex smiled back at her and quickly prepared for bed. He decided to wear a pair of jogging pants. He usually didn't wear anything to bed, but he didn't want to startle Mariam.

Mariam smiled when she came back and saw Alex in his jogging pants, but she didn't say anything. She went over and turned back the covers and climbed into the bed. She moved over so Alex would have plenty of room and lay back and waited.

Alex turned off the lights and made his way over to the bed. He settled in beside Mariam. He turned toward her and gently lifted her and put his arm behind her. He drew her close, so her head was on his chest.

"Good night, Love," he said, kissing the top of her head.

"Good night, Alex. I love you," said Mariam.

Alex held her close, and they both closed their eyes and tried to sleep. They were soon both sleeping soundly, safe in each other's arms.

Mariam awakened the next morning and lay quietly, looking around. She felt safe in Alex's arms. She moved her head slightly and looked up at Alex. His eyes were open, and he smiled at her.

"Good morning," said Alex softly.

"Good morning, have you been awake long?" asked Mariam

"A little while; I have been enjoying holding you and knowing you are safe in my arms," said Alex.

Mariam started to move, then she realized she was lying with an arm and leg over Alex. She had snuggled closer while she was sleeping. Her long tee-shirt had inched up while she was sleeping, and her bare leg was thrown over Alex's legs. She started to move away, but Alex tightened his arms around her and held her still.

"We need to get up and get ready before Andrew or Charles comes looking for us," said Mariam as she relaxed in Alex's arms.

"I know," agreed Alex. "Just a few more minutes. I don't want to move. I haven't felt so rested since I first started looking for you. I want to savor the closeness."

"I know what you mean," said Mariam. "I was beginning to think I would never feel safe again, but in your arms, I slept deeply."

"I hope this is the start of many years sleeping in my arms," said Alex. "Will you marry me as soon as I can make arrangements?"

"Yes," answered Mariam.

Alex kissed her, and Mariam held him close and kissed him back.

"Do you have any family to invite?" asked Mariam.

"No, it is just me and Mark, and since Mark and Darrin are both on their way overseas, I see no reason to wait," said Alex.

"No reason at all," agreed Mariam.

After another very satisfying kiss, Alex groaned.

"We have to get up," he whispered.

"Yes," agreed Mariam, placing small kisses along his jawline.

"You are not making it any easier," said Alex.

Mariam grinned up at him. "One of us has to be the strong one," she said. "I elect you." She kissed his chin lightly.

Alex groaned. "I don't want to be strong. I want to

take you to city hall and find a justice of the peace and then make you mine so we can stay in bed for a couple of weeks while someone else takes care of business," said Alex.

"That sounds like a plan," said Mariam. "What are we waiting for? Let's go take care of Sara's dad so we can put your plan into action."

Alex kissed her one more time before pulling free and getting out of bed. The covers pulled back when he rose. He looked over and enjoyed the view of Mariam's long bare legs. Mariam grinned at his appreciative look and climbed out of bed, letting her long tee-shirt fall into place, covering most of her legs.

"Spoilsport," remarked Alex softly.

Mariam just grabbed her clothes and headed for the bathroom to shower and change.

Alex grabbed a change of clothes and went next door to Mariam's room to shower and change.

When he finished and went to his room to leave his jogging pants, Mariam was waiting for him, already dressed. He pulled her into his arms and kissed her before taking her hand and going down the stairs in search of food.

Charles and Andrew were already in the kitchen, along with Charles' housekeeper, Mrs. Dory.

"Good morning," said Mariam with a smile at everyone.

"Good morning," said Charles. "This is my housekeeper, Mrs. Dory."

Alex and Mariam smiled and nodded at Mrs. Dory.

"Sit down," said Mrs. Dory. "I'll bring you coffee. The food is on the counter. I'll let you fix your own plates with what you like."

She went to get coffee. Mariam and Alex went to the counter, and, picking up a plate, each started filling the plate with food. There were scrambled eggs, bacon, sausage, pancakes, biscuits, hash browns, and several kinds of jellies there.

"My goodness, you could feed an army," said Mariam.

"After breakfast," said Charles, "Mrs. Dory packs up what is left over and takes it to the local homeless shelter."

"What a wonderful idea," said Mariam.

"I only do it a couple of times a week. There are other ladies from our church taking care of other days," said Mrs. Dory.

"I think it is a wonderful idea," said Mariam. "It's great for you to help out with expenses, Charles. I know all of the food costs you."

"I don't mind," said Charles. "My mom started the homeless shelter years ago. She couldn't stand the sight of people sleeping on the street."

"It would be good if other towns followed your example," said Alex.

"Our church works with the homeless to try and find them jobs and places to live, so they won't be homeless anymore," said Mrs. Dory. "The only problem is, every time we almost have all of them situated, more show up. They hear about our town and come looking for us."

Everyone smiled at Mrs. Dory's disgruntled look.

"I can see why Mercy fits this town," said Mariam. "Ever since I have arrived here, this town has welcomed me."

"We do our best," said Mrs. Dory.

"Do you know the Mayor, Mr. Talcove?" asked Alex.

"Him," sniffed Mrs. Dory. "Everyone knows him. He only got elected because he married Miss Lana. Everyone in town loves Miss Lana."

Alex grinned. "I take it you don't care for him."

"He just rubs me the wrong way," said Mrs. Dory. "I don't know anything against him. I just don't like him."

Alex nodded. "We all have people we don't like, and sometimes we don't understand why."

"Yes," agreed Mrs. Dory. "It's just a feeling."

"Always listen to your feelings. Sometimes a strong feeling can save your life," said Alex.

"I'll go straighten up upstairs while you all finish your breakfast," said Mrs. Dory.

"Thank you, Mrs. Dory," said Charles.

Mrs. Dory nodded and hurried away.

"Why did you ask her about Woodrow?" asked Charles.

"Sometimes people will say or do things, in front of the help, they wouldn't say or do in front of others," said Alex.

"They don't think these people matter, so they are not careful."

Charles nodded. "I can understand. I have seen Woodrow look through Mrs. Dory as if she were not there. He has a whole different demeanor when he is around anyone he considers his equal," said Charles.

"How are we going to get Mr. Mayor to a place where we can work on him?" asked Andrew.

"Charles, do you think you could get him to have lunch with you?" asked Alex. "If he would meet you at the bookstore, we could take it from there."

"I'll see what I can do," said Charles.

Charles dialed Woodrow's number and waited for an answer.

"Hello," said Woodrow.

"Hello, Woodrow, this is Charles. I was wondering if we could have lunch today. I have some town business I would like to discuss with you."

"Alright, Charles, would one o'clock be okay?" asked Woodrow.

"It is fine. Would the café next to Grandma's bookstore be okay?" asked Charles.

"It will be fine. You want me to meet you there?" asked Woodrow.

"Could you meet me in the bookstore? I need to check on Grandma," said Charles.

"Okay, Charles, I'll see you at one," said Woodrow.

They both hung up, and Charles grinned at Alex. "He will be at the bookstore at one."

Alex nodded and reached for his phone.

"Hello, Trey, could you be at the bookstore by 12:30? Mr. Talcove is going to be there at one, and I want to be sure we have him covered if he decides to come early," said Alex.

"Thanks, Trey,"

Alex hung up his phone and grinned at the others.

"He and Lori will be there. Sal and Micky have already left," said Alex.

Charles' phone rang. He looked at the screen and then answered.

"Hello, Kenny, is everything okay?" asked Charles.

"Everything is fine. Darci wants to know if it is okay to open the bookstore," said Kenny.

"Tell her to open up, but keep the inventory sign up and tell her to bring Sammy with her," said Charles.

"I thought we caught everyone last night," said Kenny.

"All but one, the boss is still out there. We are going to take care of him today," said Charles.

"Who is he?" asked Kenny.

"Woodrow Talcove," said Charles.

"The Mayor!" exclaimed Kenny.

"Yes," agreed Charles.

"Can we think up a punishment for him to add into his reprogramming? After all, he is getting away with a lot of things he has been responsible for these last ten years," remarked Kenny.

"I'll talk to Alex and Trey and see if we can come up with something," said Charles.

Charles hung up and grinned at Alex.

Kenny wants to know if we can come up with a way to punish Woodrow for all the grief he has caused the last ten years," said Charles.

Alex looked thoughtful. "Do you have any ideas?" he asked.

Charles looked thoughtful. "There are two boys whose mother and father died in a car crash eight years ago. It was speculated that witch hunters had something to do with it, but I could never prove it. They were adopted into a family outside of town. One of them is ready for college, and the other one will be ready next year. We could have Woodrow set up a college fund for them and contribute a healthy sum into it and ask for donations and arrange grants for them. It won't make up for losing their parents, but it will give them a start on a better future," said Charles.

"Great, I'm all for helping young people get a better start," said Mariam.

"If we can make it work, we will help the boys, too," said Alex. "They will need an allowance for clothes and other things."

Mariam hugged and kissed him. When she drew back, Andrew and Charles were both grinning at them.

Mariam flushed slightly at their attention.

"Mariam and I are going to be married when we settle Woodrow. We thought maybe the city hall. You do have a Justice of the Peace, don't you?" asked Alex. He drew Mariam close to his side.

"Yes, congratulations," said Charles. "We can handle the wedding after we see to Woodrow."

"Yes," agreed Alex. "Let's get to the bookstore and get things ready."

They all gathered their things. Alex and Mariam put their clothes back into Alex's duffle bag, which he stowed in the trunk of his car.

They followed Charles and Andrew back to the bookstore. They parked in back of the bookstore so their cars were not visible from the street. They went inside to find Darci, Sammy, and Kenny waiting for them.

CHAPTER 11

Mariam smiled at Darci. Darci looked at Mariam's glowing face and smiled back.

"What's going on?" asked Kenny.

"We are going to shut down the witch hunters in Mercy once and for all," said Charles.

"How are you going to handle it?" asked Darci.

"We are working on it," said Alex. "We are waiting on Lori and Trey. We will talk to Trey and see what we can do."

"When Trey and Lori arrive, Charles can join them in the break room, and you all can be sitting around drinking a cup of coffee. Kenny, you can stay out here with Darci and Sammy. I'll stay with Mariam and help her with counting the books," said Alex. "When Woodrow arrives, he will ask for Charles. Darci, you can send him to the break room. When he gets there, Charles will introduce Trey and Lori. Lori has a ring that will give him a slight dose of sleeping potion when he shakes hands."

Alex stopped and looked around.

"He will start to feel dizzy. Charles will help him sit, and then Trey can work on him," said Alex.

"I hope we don't have any problems with him," said Darci.

Kenny put an arm around her and reassured her. "He is just a man. He projects an image to make himself seem larger than life, but it is all a cover-up so he can control others and make them do his dirty work for him."

"I know you are right," nodded Darci. "But I hate the idea of his twisted beliefs being in touch with Sara. She is such a loving, good-hearted child. I don't want him to mess up her childhood."

"He won't," promised Charles. "We found out in time and any damage he has done we have time to correct. Sara and Lana will be fine."

Charles eyed his grandma standing comfortably with Kenny's arm around her. He smiled. It looked like Darci was becoming softer where Kenny was concerned. He was glad. He wanted Darci to be happy, and he had a feeling Kenny would make her happy.

There was a knock at the back door, and Alex went to let Trey and Lori in.

After all the greetings, Alex explained to Trey what they planned on doing with Woodrow and how they wanted to have him help the boys go to college.

Trey nodded agreement. He was all for Woodrow making amends.

"Did you bring your ring?" Alex asked Lori.

Lori smiled. "It's right here," said Lori, raising her hand.

"You guys need to get in the break room and get ready. Woodrow may show up early," said Darci.

"You are right," agreed Charles as he led the way to the break room and started the coffee.

While Trey, Lori, and Charles settled into the break room, Kenny and Darci stayed at the counter with Sammy standing watch beside Darci. Alex and Mariam wandered the bookshelves pretending to do inventory.

At five minutes to one, Darci and Kenny looked toward the front door as Woodrow entered. They did not move; they stayed where they were and waited for Woodrow to approach them.

"Hello, Mrs. Holt," said Woodrow. "Is Charles here? He asked me to meet him here."

Darci nodded. "Hello, Woodrow, Charles is in the break room talking to some friends. You can go on back."

"Thank you," said Woodrow with a smile as he headed for the break room. He passed by Mariam and Alex with a nod in their direction but did not speak.

Woodrow entered the break room with a smile for Charles. He looked around at Lori and Trey and nodded.

Charles and Trey stood when he entered, but Lori stayed seated.

"Hello, Woodrow," said Charles. "Thank you for meeting me. These are some friends of mine. They are paying me a short visit while they are passing through town. This is Trey Loden and his wife, Lori."

Trey reached over and shook Woodrow's hand, and Lori extended her hand for Woodrow to shake. He had to lean over to shake Lori's hand, and when he did, he felt a slight sting as if something bit him.

"I'm pleased to meet you," said Woodrow, licking his finger where he had felt the sting.

"It's nice to meet some of Charles' family," said

Trey. "We have been friends for a while, but this is the first time we have managed to come by for a visit.

"Sit down for a minute, Woodrow. We have a few minutes before we have to go," said Charles. He pulled out a chair for Woodrow, and when he sat down, Charles and Trey sat down also.

"Would you like some coffee?" asked Lori.

"No, thank you," said Woodrow. He shook his head as if to clear his sight.

By licking his finger, he had made the sleeping potion work faster. A moment later, he started slumping in his chair. Charles caught him before he could fall, and Trey brought forth a rope and tied him to his chair.

Trey, Charles, and Lori formed a circle around Woodrow while Trey closed his eyes and communicated with Woodrow's guardian angel.

A moment later, Trey opened his eyes. "We are going to need some help," he said. "Woodrow has built a mental wall to keep his guardian angel out. He thought he was being attacked by a witch when he heard his guardian angel's voice when he was small. So, he built the wall to keep her out. We have to take down the wall or at least open it, and we need more help."

Charles went to the door and called the others in, Andrew had joined the group, and he came, too.

"Darci, you need to lock the front door so we won't be interrupted," said Charles.

Darci hurried over and locked the front door, and then hurried back to join them in the break room.

Everyone waited for Trey to explain why they were called back to help.

"I needed your guardian angels' help," he said.

"We have to dismantle a mental wall so the guardian angels can talk to Woodrow. With all of us together, we can do it. Make a circle around Woodrow and hold hands."

Charles pulled Woodrow's chair out from the table more so they could form a circle around him. They all joined hands and waited for Trey to start.

Trey closed his eyes and concentrated. "Good, one block at a time," he said softly. Trey smiled, and everyone relaxed a little. "Keep on. You are almost done," said Trey. "Now, let's talk to Woodrow, Angels. There are no such things as witches. You have a guardian angel looking out for you. Witches do not exist. You are safe, and you want to help others.

"You want to set up a college fund for the Janos brothers. You will open it with a good donation and ask for more donations from townspeople. You will find them grants and scholarships to help them through college. You will not remember this talk. All you will remember is meeting Charles' friends and going to lunch with him and setting up the fund for the Janos brothers. He wanted to talk to you about providing more parking for Darci's bookstore. You promised to look into it and get back to him. When you wake up, you will thank Charles for lunch and go to your office and get started on setting up the college fund for the Janos brothers. Remember, there is no such thing as a witch. You have a guardian angel, and you will listen to her and be guided by her."

Trey sat back and opened his eyes. "Thanks, Angels," he said and smiled.

Everyone dropped hands and smiled in relief.

"Everyone, scatter before he wakes up," said Trey.

They all left the room quickly, all except Trey,

Charles, and Lori. Trey took the rope from around Woodrow, and they all sat down and pretended to be drinking coffee.

Darci went and unlocked the front door, and then they waited to see what would happen.

Woodrow stirred and opened his eyes. He looked around at the others, confused for a minute. Charles looked at him and smiled.

"I appreciate you looking into the parking problem at Darci's bookstore," said Charles.

Woodrow stood and paused for a minute to get his balance. "I had better get back to the office. Thanks for lunch, Charles. By the way, I have been thinking about setting up a fund so the Janos boys can go to college. If you will spread the word, I'll have the bank handle it."

"Sure, that is a good idea. We need to be sure our young people get a good start in life," agreed Charles. "I'll do what I can to help."

"Thanks," said Woodrow. He looked at Trey and Lori. "It was nice to meet you folks. I hope you enjoy your visit."

"I'm sure we will. It was nice to meet you," said Lori.

Trey nodded and got up to shake his hand. Woodrow shook hands and left. He passed by Darci and Kenny with a nod and hurried away.

Charles came out of the break room and joined Kenny and Darci at the counter.

"It worked," said Darci with a big smile.

"Yes, we should not have any more problems with witch hunters in Mercy," said Charles. He turned to look at Alex and Mariam.

"I am so glad you picked our town to hide in,"

Charles told Mariam.

"So am I," agreed Mariam. She smiled up at Alex by her side. "I'm even happier Alex found me."

"So am I," agreed Alex. He looked around at the group. "Thank you all for helping."

"That's what you pay us the big bucks for," joked Andrew. He smiled and looked at Trey and Lori. "Would you like to come with Mariam and me to the Justice of the Peace and watch us get married before you leave?" he asked.

Lori squealed and hugged Mariam. Mariam smiled as she hugged her back.

"I think she means yes," agreed Trey with a smile as he shook Alex's hand and congratulated him.

"We can go ahead and set things up," said Charles. "I know Darci and Lori will want to help Mariam get ready."

"I'll see you in a little while," said Alex as he kissed her and reluctantly went with Charles and Trey to get everything ready.

Darci sent Kenny to take Sammy to his house while she and Lori took Mariam down to the resale shop to look for a dress. Mariam flatly refused to spend a lot of money on a new dress.

"I'll be able to use my bank account after I leave here, and I will have to buy new clothes.' For now, let's see what we can find," said Mariam.

They went into the store and looked around. Mariam spotted a line of negligees and started for them. One, in particular, caught her eye. She touched it. It was soft and almost see-through. It was a lovely shade of aqua. Mariam took it down and checked to see it was her size. Mariam held on to it as she looked around for Darci and Lori. She found them going through some dresses.

Lori looked at what Mariam was carrying and smiled. "I see you found a very important part of the wedding night," said Lori.

Darci looked at the gown and smiled. "It's lovely," she said.

Darci pulled forth a semi-formal off-white gown. It was a very beautiful gown and the right size. "Is there somewhere I can try this on?" asked Mariam.

"There is a room at the back," said Darci.

Mariam and Lori followed Darci to the back to a dressing room. Mariam went inside and tried on the dress. It fit perfectly. Mariam stepped out so the others could see the dress.

Darci and Lori started nodding as soon as she stepped out.

"It is perfect," said Lori.

"It looks as if it was made for you," said Darci.

Mariam gazed in the mirror and looked at Lori.

"Lori, call Trey and see if they have made arrangements for the wedding," said Mariam.

Lori took out her phone and placed a call to Trey.

"Hi, Love," said Trey.

"Hi, we were wondering if arrangements have been made for the wedding," said Lori.

"Yes, Alex asked the Justice of the Peace if he would perform the ceremony at the bookstore in two hours. He said yes, and Alex has a marriage license. So, I guess we are all set," said Trey. "Are you ladies all set?"

"Yes, we found a dress. We'll see you in two hours," said Lori.

She hung up the phone and turned to Darci and

Mariam. "Trey said Alex has the license and the Justice of the Peace is going to meet us at the bookstore in two hours to perform the ceremony," said Lori.

Darci smiled. "We need to get back there and do a little decorating."

"Let me get out of this dress, and we can go," said Mariam.

Mariam changed clothes and paid for both outfits, and they headed for the bookstore.

When they arrived, Darci shooed Mariam back to her room to get ready and kept Lori with her to help decorate. After Mariam was gone, Darci called a friend at the local flower shop and asked her to bring over all the flowers she could spare. She promised her friend she could have the flowers back after the wedding.

The flowers started arriving a short time later. They were brought over by her friend's teenage grandson. He helped Lori arrange them around the bookstore. They moved the table to one side so there was room for Mariam and Alex and friends to stand.

Everything was coming together well. Darci and Lori looked around with satisfaction. For such short notice, it looked great.

Lori headed for the back to see if she could help Mariam.

"Come in," called Mariam when Lori knocked on her door.

Lori entered and found Mariam, fresh from a shower, sitting in front of her mirror in a robe. She had fixed her hair and was working on her makeup.

"Did you two finish decorating?" asked Mariam.

"Yes, the place looks lovely," said Lori. "I wanted

to tell you how happy I am you are marrying Alex," said Lori. "I have dreaded the time when he found someone. I was afraid he would find someone who wouldn't want me around. I could have always stayed home and let Trey go alone, but I really like us being together. I know when the baby comes, I will have to stay home more, but at the time I didn't know I could have children. Anyway, I am glad Alex found you and you are joining our family, because we are a family, even if not by blood."

Mariam stood and hugged her. "I am glad you all have accepted me into your family. I lost my family, all but my brother, and I was feeling very lost. With all the love I have been shown from you all, I am not feeling lost anymore," said Mariam.

Mariam and Lori hugged one more time, and then Mariam turned toward where her dress was laid out on her bed. "I guess I need to get dressed," said Mariam. "I wouldn't want to keep Alex waiting."

"When he sees you, he will know it was worth the wait," said Lori.

Mariam smiled and stepped into her dress. She pulled it up and turned for Lori to button it for her.

"All ready," said Lori. "I'll go see if Alex and the others are ready."

Lori left, and Mariam looked in the mirror and smiled.

"Your sister is very happy, Darrin. Thank you for sending the love of my life to find me," said Mariam.

CHAPTER 12

*L*ori came back to tell her everything was ready and Darci had borrowed a player so she could play music when Mariam was ready.

Mariam smiled mistily. Darci had been a good friend to her from the moment they had met. She was going to miss her.

They heard the music start to play, and Lori and Mariam left her room and started for the front of the bookstore. When they entered the room, they found Alex and Trey standing talking to an elderly gentleman at the front of the store. Charles, Andrew, Kenny, and Darci were standing around listening.

Darci glanced up and smiled as she saw Mariam.

Alex noticed the attention was focused behind him and turned to look. He caught his breath and smiled at the vision walking toward him. Mariam smiled back at him and stopped at his side. Alex took her hand and squeezed it.

"You look beautiful," he whispered.

"Thanks," said Mariam smiling mistily while looking into his eyes.

The Justice of the Peace cleared his throat to bring the attention back to him.

"Are we ready to start?" he asked, smiling at Mariam.

Mariam smiled and nodded.

"We are ready," said Alex.

The Justice read the vows and performed the wedding and the ring exchange with everyone listening and nodding happily. After he finished and they exchanged a kiss, he had Alex and Mariam sign the license. Next, he had Lori and Trey sign as witnesses, and then he signed and stamped it. He took a copy with him to file at the courthouse and gave a copy to Alex. When all the business was done, everyone crowded around to congratulate Alex and Mariam.

"This isn't over," said Darci.

Alex and Mariam looked at her curiously.

"I arranged for a reception to be held in the café next door. They should be ready for us, so let's go on over," said Darci.

Darci took Alex and Mariam by the hands and started for the door. Everyone followed them, including the Justice of the Peace.

When they entered the café, Mariam gasped and gazed around in surprise. Everyone there smiled and clapped their hands for the bride and groom.

"It's beautiful," Mariam said. She smiled mistily at everyone and held onto Alex's arm tightly as she looked around at people of town who had become friends while she had been a member of their town.

Flowers decorated each table, and on a front table was a large wedding cake. An area at the back had been cleared for a small dance floor. Some of the residents from town were also there. Many of them had met Mariam at the bookstore and liked her.

Mariam turned to Darci and hugged her. "You didn't have to do this, but I love it," she said.

Darci hugged her back. "I have come to feel like you are my family. I wanted to make sure you had a memorable day."

Alex grinned and hugged Darci. "Thank you," he said.

"That's not all," said Darci. "I have been staying with Kenny, so I had some ladies go in and clean my house and change the sheets so you will have a nice place for your wedding night."

She handed the key and a note with directions to her house to Alex.

Alex took it and hugged her again.

"Do you mind if I adopt you as my Grandmother?" asked Alex.

Darci flushed with pleasure. "It will be my honor," she said.

Mariam hugged her again. "Thanks," she said.

"Let's cut the cake," said Darci turning to the cake to hide her misty eyes. Kenny came up beside her and put an arm around her. Darci leaned into him slightly as if for support.

They all gathered around the cake. Alex and Mariam took the knife and held it together while someone took a picture. Then, they made the first cut. Alex took a small piece and fed it to Mariam as she fed him a small bite. They handed the knife over to the ladies and moved away as the cake was cut and handed around.

Alex and Mariam made their way to the dance

floor and stood swaying to the music. Alex kissed her and held her close.

"You are mine," he whispered.

"Yes, and you are mine," agreed Mariam. "I am so glad you came looking for me. I'm going to have to do something nice for Darrin and Mark."

"We can throw them a big party when they return from overseas," said Alex.

"I'll think about it," said Mariam. She smiled up into Alex's eyes. "I have other things on my mind right now."

"There is food on the counter so everyone can serve yourselves," called out Darci.

Trey and Lori joined Alex and Mariam on the dance floor. Kenny caught Darci's hand and drew her into a dance, also. When the music stopped, they all went to fix themselves a plate of food, and when they sat down, the waitress went around giving everyone a glass of champagne. They started eating their food; but waited until everyone was served before drinking their champagne.

"Let's everyone raise our glasses to the nicest couple I know," said Trey. "To Alex and Mariam, may they enjoy many years of happiness and be glad they listened to Love's Voice and found each other."

"To Alex and Mariam," echoed everyone as they raised their glasses to drink.

Charles stood and raised his glass. "Thank you both for honoring our town with your presence. I wish you every happiness and hope we see a lot more of you."

"Hear, hear," said Darci and Kenny.

Kenny stood and raised his glass. "I want to thank you both for coming to our town and helping me to convince the love of my life to give us a chance. Without you, I would still be on the outside hoping for a chance. To Alex and Mariam."

Everyone laughed as they echoed his words and drank again. Kenny sat down and captured Darci's hand and gave it a gentle squeeze.

Alex stood. They all quieted and looked at him. He smiled at the people around the table. "Mariam and I have made new friends in this town. We are thankful for every one of you. We will never be able to thank you enough for the love and support you have shown to us as strangers in your town. You have become friends and family. We will never forget you, and you can be sure you will be hearing from us. I am going to be sure Charles and Darci have our numbers, so if there is ever a need, you can call on us and we will be there for you."

There was many a misty eye when Alex sat down and put his arm around Mariam and kissed her.

Everyone concentrated on eating, laughing, and talking with each other. Trey and Lori were seated beside Alex. Trey leaned forward and talked to Alex. Lori smiled at Mariam, as she leaned back so the two guys could talk.

"Lori and I are going to spend the night in the motel. We were planning to leave first thing in the morning. Do you want us to wait for you so we can travel together?" asked Trey.

"If you have room, I can turn in my rental car, and we can ride with you," said Alex.

Alex looked at Mariam. "Is it okay with you, or would you rather fly?" asked Alex.

"I would love to travel with Trey and Lori," said

Mariam. "Lori can fill me in on what to expect when we reach our destination."

"We have plenty of room," said Lori. "I would love a chance to get to know Mariam better."

"Okay, we will wait for you in the morning and then go by the rental place at the airport and turn in your car," agreed Trey.

"Good," said Alex with a nod. He looked at Mariam. He took her hand and helped her up. "We will have one more dance and then say goodbye to everyone."

He led her to the dance floor and drew her into his arms. They danced until the music stopped, then went in search of Darci to say goodbye. They found Darci and Kenny by the food counter. They were talking, and it looked like Kenny had finally managed to convince Darci to take a chance on him.

Mariam hugged Darci and told her their plans. "We are going to leave now. You all can stay here and enjoy our party. Thank you so much for all you have done for me since the first day we met. You gave me a job and a home and showed me there are people in the world who care. I love you, Darci, and I will keep in touch." She looked at Kenny. "You take good care of my grandmother, Kenny. She is one in a million."

"Yes, Ma'am," said Kenny. Mariam went over and hugged him, also. When she drew away, Kenny was misty-eyed.

Alex hugged Darci and shook hands with Kenny.

"I meant what I said," said Alex. "If you ever need us, just call."

"We will," promised Darci returning his hug.

Alex and Mariam slipped out of the café and went to Alex's car. Everyone was having a good time and did not pay any attention to them leaving. Kenny led Darci out to the dance floor and held her while they swayed to the music. Lori and Trey had packed what clothes Mariam had in her room and put them in Alex's car. Lori knew Mariam would want her new negligee.

Alex followed Darci's directions and was soon stopping in front of Darci's house. He stopped the car and helped Mariam out of the car. Mariam reached into the back seat to retrieve her shopping bag. Alex took her hand, guiding her to the front door. He used Darci's key to open the door. Turning, he swung Mariam up into his arms.

"Shouldn't we wait until we arrive at our new home before you carry me over the threshold?" asked Mariam.

Alex kissed her. "I'll carry you over again when we get home," said Alex. "I may carry you over each new threshold we come to." He carried her inside and kissed her again.

"I need to go and change out of this dress," said Mariam.

"Do you need any help?" asked Alex huskily.

"No, I have a surprise for you," said Mariam. She looked around. "Which way is the bedroom?"

"I don't know, but I'm sure we can find it," said Alex. They started down the hall, checking out rooms as they went. The bedroom was at the end of the hall. They opened the door and turned on the light. Mariam turned and kissed Alex as she encouraged him out the door. "Just a few minutes, I'll call you," said Mariam as she shut the door.

Mariam opened her bag and took out her negligee. Removing her dress, she hung it carefully over a chair. After slipping on the negligee, Mariam turned and looked in the mirror.

She flushed slightly, but she loved the way she looked. She turned sideways and looked again.

Mariam went to the door and opened it. She didn't know Alex was waiting just outside of the door. Alex stepped inside the room. He gazed at Mariam, then drew her into his arms and kissed her deeply.

"I didn't think you could be any more beautiful," he whispered huskily.

"You have on too many clothes," teased Mariam softly.

Alex pulled back and started peeling off clothes. "Not for long." He was soon shed of his wedding clothes and helped Mariam pull the negligee over her head. He was very careful with it. "I want you to wear this for me again when we are at home," said Alex.

"Okay," agreed Mariam. She wasn't really paying any attention to what they were saying. She was all about feeling and how wonderful it felt to be making love to Alex.

"Oh my," said her guardian angel.

"You go take a hike," said Mariam.

"What?" asked Alex drawing back slightly and looking puzzled.

"I was talking to my peeping tom guardian angel," said Mariam.

Alex grinned and started kissing her again.

They were soon so absorbed in each other they wouldn't have noticed a dozen guardian angels.

CHAPTER 13

*A*fter a wonderful night of making love, Mariam and Alex were straightening Darci's house and changing the bed. They wanted to leave it in good condition. Mariam made them breakfast while the sheets were washing. They were ready to leave when Alex's phone rang.

"Hello, Charles, we are just about to leave," said Alex.

"We have some visitors at the station," said Charles. "I was called to come in. There are two FBI agents there looking for Mariam."

"Are you sure they are FBI?" asked Alex.

"I checked them out. They said they need to ask Mariam about the fire and her family's death," said Charles.

Alex turned and looked at Mariam.

"Charles said there are two FBI agents at the station. They want to ask you some questions about the fire," said Alex.

Mariam paled. She took a deep breath and squared her shoulders. "We have to go and talk to them. I am through running," she said.

Alex took her hand and squeezed it. "We will be there shortly, Charles," said Alex.

They hung up the phone. They carried the clothes they had brought in with them the night before and put them in the trunk of the car. Alex opened the car door for Mariam, then ran back and locked the door. Alex called Trey and filled him in and asked him to wait until they knew what was going on before leaving. Alex gave Mariam a reassuring hand squeeze and smile before starting for the police station.

"Don't worry. No way am I going to let anything happen to you," he promised. Mariam smiled and squeezed his hand.

They were soon walking into the police station. Charles saw them and motioned for them to follow him to his office. The two agents were already in his office waiting. They both stood when Mariam and Alex entered the room.

"Alex, Mariam, this are Agents Slocome and Hatch. Gentlemen, this is Mr. and Mrs. Alex Avorn," said Charles.

Mariam grinned at Charles. She loved hearing her new name.

Both agents held out hands for them to shake. Alex and Mariam then took their seats. The agents sat back down, and Charles sat behind his desk.

"Avorn, as in Avorn Security?" asked one of the agents.

"Yes," agreed Alex with a nod.

"It's nice to meet you. Our boss has a high regard for you," he said.

"Yeah," said the other agent. "He asked us just the other day why we had so much trouble solving cases and why Avorn Security was solving them before us."

Alex smiled. "We get a lucky break sometimes."

Agent Hatch looked dubious, like he wasn't sure if Alex was right.

"What did you want to talk to my wife about?" asked Alex.

The agents looked at Mariam. "We are sorry to have to bother you, Ma'am, but we are trying to find out about the fire where your family died. The local police ruled it an accident, but we have reason to believe it was not an accident," said the agent.

"The fire was not an accident. It was arson," said Alex.

"How do you know?" asked Agent Slocome.

"Darrin, Mariam's brother, asked me to look around. I looked around the burn site. Gas was poured around the house and garage. Then someone broke in and poured gas all around downstairs. They lit the downstairs on fire and then went outside and set fire outside. It was set deliberately," explained Alex.

"Did you tell the local police your findings?" asked Agent Hatch.

"No, Darrin had tried to get them to help him find out what had happened and where Mariam was. They were not interested in helping," said Alex.

"Is that when he asked you to help?" asked Agent Hatch.

"Yes," said Alex. "Darrin is a friend of my brother. They are in the same regiment. My brother asked me to help."

"Why did you leave, Mrs. Avorn?" asked Agent Slocome.

"Because someone was trying to kill me," said Mariam.

The agents looked startled. "Why were they trying to kill you?" Agent Hatch asked.

"They thought I was a witch," said Mariam.

"Are you a witch?" asked Agent Slocome.

Mariam looked at the agent sharply. "Of course not, there is no such thing as witches." Mariam looked at Agent Slocome sharply. "You don't believe in witches, do you, Agent?"

"No, Ma'am, but there are some nutcases out there who do believe in them," he said.

"I know," said Mariam with a shiver. "They tried to kill me several times."

"Why didn't you go to the police for help?" asked Agent Hatch.

"I don't know," said Mariam. "I started to, but I just felt I couldn't trust them to protect me."

"Why are you asking all of these questions?" asked Alex.

"We have had some complaints about the police department in Madison. Yours is not the only fire they have called an accident. We think something is going on in the town, and the police department is right in the middle of it," said Agent Hatch.

Agent Hatch looked at Alex. "We are not supposed to talk about our cases, but since you already know about it, I don't see the harm. If you tell my boss I told you, I will deny it."

Alex laughed. "I won't tell anyone. I never heard you say a word."

Mariam looked at him and grinned. They all turned and looked at Charles. Charles raised his hands. "I'm just a small-town deputy sheriff. I haven't heard a thing," he said with a grin. Both agents turned back to Alex. They were satisfied with Charles' reaction.

Before they could say anything else, the door burst open and a man came into Charles' office. Charles stood. "Agent Franks, it is customary to knock before entering my office."

"I heard there were FBI agents here," said Agent Franks.

"Did you damage your hand hurrying over here, so you couldn't knock? I can't see how my visitors are any of your business," said Charles.

Mariam turned pale and was very still. She looked at Alex and slightly shook her head. Alex looked at Mariam and then looked at Agent Franks.

"It's customary for agents to check in with the local office when they are in town on an investigation," said Agent Franks.

"Agent Slocome and Agent Hatch are not here on a case," said Alex. "They stopped to pass a message to me from their boss. He is a friend of mine."

Agent Hatch and Agent Slocome looked at Alex, startled. Then they looked at Agent Franks.

Charles looked at Alex with narrowed eyes. He turned to Agent Franks and gave him a stern look. "If you don't mind, Agent Franks, we are busy. Would you excuse us? If you have any business to discuss with me, make an appointment with the desk, and I will get back to you as soon as I can."

Agent Franks turned and left, leaving the door open. Alex got up and shut it.

Alex came back over and took Mariam's hands. "Are you alright?"

"Yes, I'm fine. I just didn't like his attitude," said Mariam.

"Are there any more questions for my wife?" asked Alex.

"No," said Agent Hatch. "I don't think Mrs. Avorn can help us. You be careful, Ma'am. If you have any more trouble, you get in touch with us. We will do our best to help you."

Mariam smiled at them. "Thank you, Agent Hatch. I will remember your kindness."

The agents stood. Alex and Charles both stood and shook hands with them. Then Charles showed them out and shut the door.

Alex looked at Mariam and waited. "It was my guardian angel. She said Agent Franks was bad," said Mariam. Charles shook his head and sat back down.

"I should have remembered," he said. "Woodrow and Agent Franks were buddies. They hung out together all the time. Agent Franks probably doesn't know about Woodrow's change of heart. I doubt they have had a chance to talk. Woodrow took Lana and Sara on a trip to visit his mom and dad. He left right after he started the fund for the Janos brothers."

"What do we do now?" asked Mariam.

"We have to neutralize Agent Franks," said Alex.

Charles shook his head. "Just when you think it is over, up pops another one," he said.

"How do we get Agent Franks alone to work on him?" asked Charles. "I can't invite him out for a meal."

"How long will Woodrow be gone?" asked Alex.

"I think he was planning on staying a week. His dad has been having health problems," said Charles.

"Do you have a key to their house?" asked Alex.

"Yes, Lana gave me one so I could feed their cat," said Charles.

"Do you think you could arrange for Woodrow's secretary to call Agent Franks and ask him to meet Woodrow at his house?" asked Alex.

Charles thought about it for a minute. "I could ask Darci to call Agent Franks' office and pretend to pass a message to Agent Franks. I don't want to get Woodrow's secretary involved. She is one of the worst gossips around here."

Alex grinned. "Whatever works."

"What excuse can Darci give to get Agent Franks to go to Woodrow's house?" asked Mariam.

"It doesn't matter what we tell him. We are going to make him forget ever being there," said Alex.

"Darci can tell him Woodrow left him instructions for their next get together. He'll think it is about the witch hunters, and he will be in a hurry to go over and get the instructions before someone else sees them," said Charles.

"I'll call Trey and get him over there, and we can all park around back, so Agent Franks won't know we are there until it's too late and he is inside," said Alex.

"Woodrow has a large garage," said Charles. "We can park inside, and Agent Franks will not know we are there."

"We need to go out to the house and get ready before Darci calls agent Franks. We don't know how long it will take for him to go there," said Alex.

"Let me call Darci, and you can call Trey," said Charles. They both took out their phones and started calling.

Mariam sat and watched them as they made the arrangements. She smiled as she watched Alex. Just looking at him made her toes curl.

Alex turned from talking to Trey and caught Mariam smiling at him. He smiled back and pulled her close and kissed her. Mariam put her hand on his face and caressed it.

"Ummm," she said. "Nice."

Charles turned and hung up his phone. He smiled at Mariam and Alex.

"I'm sorry I have to interrupt your honeymoon. Hopefully, we can wrap this up quickly and nothing else will pop up," said Charles.

"We understand," said Mariam. "We want to be sure Darci is safe before we leave."

"We don't want to take a chance on the witch hunters having someone to reorganize them," said Alex. "People like Franks can always find bored young adults who they can brainwash into doing their dirty work for them."

"Let's go to Woodrow's house. Darci and Kenny are going to meet us there. She wants to be sure we are in place before she calls Franks," said Charles.

Charles led the way, and Mariam and Alex followed him out of the police station and out to their cars. Charles then led the way to Woodrow's house.

Darci and Kenny were waiting for them when they got there.

Trey and Lori drove up as they were starting toward the house. They had Andrew with them.

"I thought you had left," Alex said to Andrew.

"I stopped to see if Trey and Lori had left, and they filled me in on what was happening. I decided to stay and see if I could help," said Andrew.

Charles had opened the garage door, and Alex and Charles drove their cars inside.

"Darci, you want to see if you can get Agent Franks?" asked Alex.

Darci called Agent Franks' number. She had already looked it up and programmed it into her phone.

"Hello, this is Darci Holt. I have a message for Agent Franks from the Mayor," said Darci.

"Just a moment," said the secretary.

"Hello, this is Agent Franks."

"Agent Franks, this is Darci Holt. My granddaughter asked me to pass a message on to you from her husband, Woodrow. They had to go out of town, suddenly, because his father is ill."

"What is the message?" asked Agent Franks impatiently.

"Woodrow wanted you to know he left you some papers about your next meeting in his study at home. He wanted you to go by and get them," said Darci.

"How am I supposed to get in? I don't have a key," said Agent Franks.

"My granddaughter left me a key to feed their cat. If you will tell me when you are going to be there, I can meet you there and let you in," said Darci.

"When can you meet me?" asked Agent Franks.

"I am here now," said Darci. "If you want to come now, I'll wait for you."

"Okay, I'll be there in a few minutes," said Agent Franks.

He hung up, and Darci turned and grinned at the others, who were watching and listening.

"He's on his way," said Darci.

"Kenny, you need to go inside with the others. I

didn't tell him you were here," said Darci. "He will expect to see one car."

"Trey, drive your car around behind the garage so it can't be seen," said Alex.

"Let's get inside and get organized," said Charles. Charles unlocked the door, and they all went inside.

"Darci, you can wait here by the door. Mariam, you and Lori go and wait in the kitchen. Charles can show us where Woodrow's office is so we can wait there," said Alex.

"Darci, you keep Sammy with you," said Charles.

Everyone scattered to do what they were told.

Mariam and Lori found the kitchen and sat on the counter stools while they waited. Charles, Alex, Trey, and Andrew went to the office. Charles hid behind the door. Andrew and Trey stood behind the curtains. Alex stood beside the bookcase. They had barely managed to hide before they heard Darci let Agent Franks in.

"Go on back, Agent Franks; I'll wait here," said Darci.

Agent Franks came through the door a minute later. He didn't look around but headed straight for the desk.

"Hold it right there," said Charles, pointing a gun at him.

"I have permission to be here," said Agent Franks, holding up his hands and turning to face Charles. While he was facing Charles, the others slipped up behind him and put the rope around him. They sat him in a chair and tied him to it.

Trey went to the door and called Lori.

Lori, Mariam, and Darci joined them in the office.

"Do you have your ring?" asked Alex.

Lori smiled, and, coming forward, she slapped Agent Franks on the shoulder.

"What did you do?" he demanded.

"You are just going to take a little nap," said Charles with a grin. Agent Franks started slumping as the sleeping potion started working on him.

Everyone stood around and held hands in a circle as Trey started talking to Agent Frank's guardian angel.

It didn't take long, and they untied Agent Franks and waited for him to wake up. When he awakened, he was confused and did not remember why he was there. Trey told him he had been inquiring about Woodrow's dad.

They promised to let Woodrow know he had been by and sent him on his way. They locked up Woodrow's house, and Trey and Lori left to take Andrew to the motel to get his car.

"We are going to miss you guys," said Mariam as she gave Darci a hug.

Alex shook Charles' hand and told him to be sure and let them know if any more witch hunters showed up. He then hugged Darci and gave her back her house key and thanked her for the use of her house, while Mariam said goodbye to Charles. They waved as they headed to the motel to meet up with Trey and Lori.

When they arrived at the motel, Andrew was getting ready to leave. They waved him off and told him they would see him at the office.

Alex transferred their luggage to the trunk of Trey's car, and they headed to the airport to turn in his car.

Alex turned in his car, and he and Mariam

climbed into the back seat of Trey's car. Alex pulled Mariam close to his side and sighed.

"Finally," he said.

Everyone laughed.

CHAPTER 14

The trip to Derring, OK, where Avorn Security was located, would take about five and a half hours. The four of them talked quietly. Lori was telling Mariam a few things about the town of Derring. Alex and Trey were discussing a new case Brenda had told them about.

They had been driving about three hours when they stopped to fill up with gas and to eat. They walked around a bit first to stretch their legs. They decided to eat there to have a break from the car.

Alex offered to drive when they continued their trip, but Trey said he was fine. So, they all settled back in the car. They had not been on the road very long when Alex glanced down at Mariam in his arms and found her fast asleep. He smiled and kissed the top of her head.

Lori looked back to say something but saw Mariam was asleep. She smiled and turned back to the front. She reached over and laid her hand on Trey's leg. Trey smiled at her and squeezed her hand tighter to his leg. He then turned his attention back to his driving.

It was very quiet in the car until they were almost at their destination. Then, Mariam stirred and blinked her eyes open. She looked up at Alex and smiled.

"I'm sorry I fell asleep on you," said Mariam.

"You needed the sleep. You have been under a lot of stress," said Alex. "I am glad you managed to relax and sleep."

"Are we almost there?" asked Mariam.

"We have about another thirty minutes," said Alex. "Trey, could we go by the airport so I can pick up my car before going home?"

"Sure," agreed Trey.

Lori looked back at Mariam and smiled. "Did you get a good sleep?" she asked.

"Yes, I feel much better now," answered Mariam, smiling and raising her face so she could kiss Alex. He tightened his arms and kissed her.

"I don't know where you live," said Mariam. "Do you have a house or an apartment?"

"I have both," said Alex. "I have a house just outside of town. Mark and I own it together, and I have a penthouse apartment over Avorn Security."

"Where will we live?" asked Mariam, widening her eyes and gazing at him.

"We are going to the apartment first. I need to check in at the office. I'll take you out to the house in a day or so, and you can decide where you want us to live."

"I get to pick?" asked Mariam.

Alex nodded. "I want you to be happy and comfortable with me wherever we are. I don't want you to regret marrying me."

Mariam leaned over and kissed him. "That will never happen," she said. "I love you."

"I love you, too," said Alex, and he kissed her again.

Trey pulled to a stop. He looked back at them and grinned.

When they looked at him confused, he laughed. "The airport," he said.

"Oh, right," said Alex, reaching in his pocket for his parking slip. He got out of the car and helped Mariam out. Trey and Lori got out, and Trey opened the trunk so they could remove their bags. Alex took the bags, and after saying thanks to Trey and Lori and promising to see them the next day at the office, Alex led the way to his car. He stowed the bags in the trunk and helped Mariam into the car. They stopped at the drive-through and paid the parking fee and then headed for the downtown office building of Avorn Security.

Mariam watched out the window as they drove; she was interested to see what her new hometown looked like.

She already knew there were some tall office and apartment buildings from her talk with Lori. They passed by a large mall on the outskirts of town. To Mariam, it was a culture shock coming into such a large town after living in Mercy. Even Madison had not been near as large a town. They passed a hospital sign pointing down a road on the left.

"Derring has its own hospital?" asked Mariam.

"Yes," said Alex. "It is a good-size hospital. I think it has four floors."

"Oh," said Mariam. She turned and looked back out the window.

Alex pulled into a parking garage under a tall office building. He pulled into a parking spot with his name on it and parked.

Mariam sat looking straight ahead at the sign. She had never known anyone who had their own parking sign with their name on it.

Alex smiled and got out and came around to help her out of the car.

He held her close and smiled at her. "I know it is not what you are used to, but you will get used to everything. Just remember, I love you. I am here for you, and I will never let anything happen to you. We will work out anything else that bothers you."

He lowered his head and kissed her. When he let her come up for air, Mariam smiled up at him. "Do you suppose I could have another one of those?" she asked.

"Anytime," said Alex, lowering his head for another kiss.

They drew apart and looked toward the sound of someone coming. Alex kept his arm around Mariam and turned toward the two gentlemen coming toward them.

"Way to go, Boss. Andrew told us you were married, but he didn't say anything about her being a looker," said one of the men.

Alex shook his head. "What are you guys doing here? I thought you were out on assignment," said Alex.

"We wrapped up and turned the case over to the locals. We found the little boy. He was with his grandma. She had taken him when she found her daughter strung out on drugs. She didn't tell his father she had him because she was afraid the boy's father would take the boy back to her daughter. The local judge has awarded her custody until the mom can prove she is drug-free," said the other man.

Alex was nodding. He looked toward Mariam. "These are two of my agents," he said. Alex pointed to one. "This is Sandore Mase – we call him Sandy. He is Sal's brother. His partner is Michael Anders. Gentlemen, this is my wife, Mariam."

"It's nice to meet you both," said Mariam.

"The pleasure is all ours," said Sandy with a big smile.

Micky just nodded and said, "Ma'am.

"I'll see you guys tomorrow," said Alex. "We were just heading upstairs."

The guys went on to their car, and Alex turned to get their bags from the trunk. The guys honked and waved as they passed back by them on the way out of the parking garage.

Alex took the bags in one hand and Mariam's hand in the other and led the way to a private elevator. He took a key and unlocked the door of the elevator, and they stepped inside. Alex punched the only button. It said "Ph" for penthouse.

"I'll get you a key for the elevator. We are the only ones who will be using it. Anyone else who wants to see us has to come through the office first and be escorted up to the penthouse," said Alex.

"Why all of the security?" asked Mariam.

"I own a security company. It would be lax of me not to make sure no disgruntled clients or others could get into my home," said Alex.

Mariam nodded. She did not know what to say.

"It will be okay," said the voice of her guardian angel.

"I know," whispered Mariam.

"What?" asked Alex.

Mariam looked up and grinned. "I was just talking to my guardian angel. She was encouraging me to relax," said Mariam.

"I'm glad she is on my side," said Alex.

"She is definitely on your side," said Mariam dryly.

The elevator stopped, and Alex dropped the bags and lifted Mariam into his arms and carried her into the living room. Alex kissed her before letting her feet down and holding her close and deepening the kiss.

"I could get used to this," said Mariam, smiling at Alex.

"Welcome to our home," said Alex.

Mariam looked around. "The front room was large and had some comfortable furniture scattered around. There was an entertainment center with a large-screen television. Over to one side was a bar with stools, and past it, she could see a kitchen and table and chairs. It was all very homey and natural. There was a large picture of an older couple and two young boys hanging over the sofa. She could tell the older boy was Alex and the younger one was Mark. *The older couple must be their parents,* she thought.

"The bedrooms are down the hall," said Alex.

"How many bedrooms are there?" asked Mariam.

"There are two and an office. Mark uses one of the bedrooms when he is here," said Alex.

Mariam nodded and followed Alex down the hall as he went to leave their bags in the bedroom.

The bedroom was large. It had a king-size bed, and there was a large-screen television in there also.

"Do you watch much television in bed?" asked Mariam.

Alex shrugged. He was getting worried. Mariam was not saying much, and he was beginning to think she did not like the apartment.

"Sometimes, I will turn on the television to catch the late news or watch a show when I can't get to sleep," he said.

He turned and put his hands on Mariam's shoulders. "If you don't like the place, we can always go out to the house, or you can redecorate here. I want you to be happy."

Mariam smiled. "I didn't mean to make you think I don't like the apartment. I think the apartment is lovely. Where we live is not as important as whom we live with. Being with you, I will be happy. I will have to get used to a very different lifestyle than I have been accustomed to, but it will all work out. My guardian angel said so," assured Mariam.

Alex drew a relieved breath and kissed her. "Lets' go see if there is anything in the fridge. I'm starved," said Alex.

He took her hand and led the way to the kitchen and the fridge. Alex opened the fridge and looked inside. Brenda had restocked it for him. Mariam glanced around him and looked inside the fridge.

"Wow," she said. "I don't think I have ever seen a fridge with so much food in it," she marveled.

"I told Brenda to buy a few things when I was talking to her yesterday," said Alex.

"You are spoiled," teased Mariam.

Alex looked at her in surprise until he saw her smile and realized she was teasing.

"I guess I am, but Brenda doesn't mind. I pay her

a very nice salary. She has two kids, and her husband left her for someone else. She was having a rough time making ends meet when she came for an interview. I hired her and soon realized what a good deal I had made. I honestly don't know how we would manage without her now. When she does me small favors, it's her way of saying thanks for giving her a chance. It should be the other way around. I should be thanking her," said Alex.

While Alex had been talking, he had been taking things out of the fridge. He set the things on the counter and went to find a pan and a bowl.

Mariam looked at the assortment of food on the counter. He had eggs, scallops, cheese, and bell peppers. Alex set the salt and pepper on the counter and laid a knife beside them. Mariam picked up the knife and started chopping the scallops and peppers and putting them in the bowl.

"How many eggs do you want?" asked Mariam.

"Six should be enough," said Alex.

Mariam cracked and added six eggs to the mix in the bowl. She added salt and pepper while Alex melted butter in a large skillet. When the butter was melted, Mariam poured the mixture into the skillet. When the omelet was cooked on one side, Mariam added the shredded cheese and folded it over to let it finish cooking and to allow the cheese melt.

Alex set out two plates and put bread in the toaster to brown. Mariam cut the omelet in half and put half on each plate. Alex brought forks and glasses of orange juice to the table.

Alex held Mariam's chair and grinned at her. "Let's eat," he said.

Mariam smiled and accepted her seat but waited

for Alex to sit before saying a brief prayer and picking up her fork.

"Ummm, this is good," said Mariam. "I must have been hungrier than I realized."

"We make a good team," said Alex.

When they finished eating, they put the dishes in the dishwasher and went into the living area. Alex sat on the sofa and pulled Mariam down onto his lap. She lay back in his arms and relaxed. Alex reached for the remote and turned the news on the television.

They both sat up with a gasp when they realized what they were seeing on the news.

"There you have it, folks," said the news reporter. "The bookstore in Mercy, Kansas, is a complete loss. There were no injuries in the fire, and the fire department kept the fire from spreading to the adjoining businesses. Two suspects believed to have started the fire were shot by the deputy sheriff. This is WLMK news signing off."

The news switched to something else, and Alex reached for his phone and called Charles.

"Hello, Alex," said Charles.

"We just saw the news. Is Darci alright?" asked Alex.

"She is fine. When those two guys came snooping around, Kenny had her lock up, and he took her to his house," said Charles.

"Do you know who they were?" asked Alex.

"According to their driver's licenses, they were from Madison, Oklahoma. One was a police officer and the other was a small-time hoodlum. I have been in touch with the police department in Madison, and they claimed they didn't know why their officer was in our town. They said he had taken some personal leave to visit a sick relative. They did not know why he was with the other man. They had been looking for the other man for suspicion of arson. There is a good chance he is the one who set fire to Mariam's home and killed her family."

"It looks like we stopped too soon," said Alex.

"Maybe now we can get past the threat of the witch hunters," said Charles. "If there was anyone they were reporting to, they know Mariam isn't here. They did not come by to talk to me. I didn't know they were here until I got the call from Kenny warning me. By the time I reached the bookstore, it was on fire and the two guys were running out with gas cans in their hands. I called for them to halt and they drew their guns. I shot them both. The police officer managed to fire, but he missed."

"I am glad you and Darci are alright. Give Darci our love, and if there is anything we can do to help, call us," said Alex.

"I will, thanks," said Charles. They hung up, and Alex turned to Mariam, who had been following the conversation from listening to Alex's side.

"Darci is fine. She was with Kenny. He heard about the guys snooping around and took her home and called Charles. Charles arrived at the bookstore and caught the men running out with gas cans. They drew on him, and he shot them both." said Alex.

"Who were they?" asked Mariam.

"One was a police officer from Madison. The other was wanted for arson. Charles thinks he may be the one to set fire to your home," said Alex.

Mariam leaned back with a sigh. "Will this ever be over? I hope I haven't brought the danger to your people."

Alex pulled her closer. "This is not your fault. I am going to have to give it some thought. We need to figure out a way to stop these people once and for all," said Alex.

Alex looked down into Mariam's face and smiled and kissed her.

"It's still early. Do you want to go down to the office with me and meet Brenda while I check in?" he asked.

"I would love to meet Brenda," said Mariam. "I think she is going to be an important part of my new life."

Alex helped her up and stood. He kissed her once more before leading her to another elevator. Once inside, he pushed the button for the third floor.

"I'll give you a tour of the building soon so you will know your way around," said Alex.

"Do you rent part of the building?" asked Mariam.

Alex shook his head. "I own the whole building, but I rent out some of it."

"You own the whole building?" gasped Mariam as the door opened and Alex drew her out of the elevator and toward a desk sitting in the lobby of the third floor offices.

CHAPTER 15

"Hello, Lynn," said Alex to the young woman sitting at the desk. "This is my wife, Mariam. Is Brenda in her office?"

"Yes, Sir. It's nice to meet you, Mrs. Avorn," greeted Lynn.

"It's nice to meet you," said Mariam as she responded to Alex's tug on her hand and followed him to an office further down the hall.

Alex knocked on the door and waited for a quiet "come in" before opening the door and entering.

Brenda looked up and gave Alex and Mariam a big smile. Mariam smiled back at her. She was surprised to see a woman around 40 sitting behind the desk. She had thought Brenda would be younger.

Brenda rose from her seat and came around her desk to shake hands with Mariam. She smiled at Alex, who was beaming with pride.

Mariam shook her head. "You did good, Boss," she said.

"I got lucky," explained Alex.

Brenda nodded. "I am happy for you both."

"Thank you," said Mariam.

"Have there been any more reports from Mercy?" asked Alex.

"Yes, Deputy Sheriff Holt called. He wanted you to know about a lawyer calling trying to locate Mrs. Avorn," said Brenda.

"Call me Mariam," said Mariam.

Brenda nodded. "I'm Brenda, I am hoping we can be friends," she said.

"I hope so, too," said Mariam.

"Did Charles say what the lawyer wanted?" asked Alex.

"He said the lawyer mentioned something about getting in touch with Mariam and her brother about their folks' life insurance and the insurance on the house that burned," said Brenda.

"I didn't know they had life insurance. I thought Darrin may have used the house insurance for the funeral," Mariam told Alex.

"I doubt he had time to collect it before he shipped out," said Alex.

"It should go to Darrin anyway. He took care of the funeral," said Mariam.

"We may have to talk to the lawyer and claim the insurance money and have it put into an account for Darrin to claim when he comes home," said Alex.

Mariam looked thoughtful.

"What is it?" asked Alex.

"What if this is all just a trick, and there are more witch hunters trying to find me?" asked Mariam.

Alex nodded. "I thought about that," he said. "We are going to have to do some investigating before we get in touch with the lawyer."

Mariam nodded. She looked at Brenda. "I hope I don't sound paranoid, but I have learned to be cautious."

"I understand," said Brenda. "I would probably be worse than you if I had those awful people looking for me."

"You don't believe in witches, do you?" asked Mariam.

Brenda laughed. "I don't know whether they exist or not, but I don't believe you are one. Alex explained about your guardian angel." Brenda held up her hand when Mariam started to speak. "We all have guardian angels. Everyone in Alex's employ is fully aware of Trey's ability to use the guardian angels to change the witch hunters from the deadly path."

Mariam smiled at Brenda's way of explaining Trey's ability.

"Is there anything urgent I need to see about?" asked Alex.

"Nothing that can't wait until morning," said Brenda. "Why don't you take your new bride down and show her around the building?"

She turned to Mariam. "There is a great spa on the second floor. I have wanted to get in there for a treatment. Maybe, after you get settled, we can go together," said Brenda.

"I would like that," said Mariam.

"We'll see you later," said Alex as he took Mariam's hand and turned toward the door. "See what you can find out about the lawyer and the insurance."

"Okay," agreed Brenda. "Just relax and enjoy your day. I'll be in touch about a spa day, Mariam."

"Thanks, I'll look forward to it," said Mariam as she and Alex left.

Alex led her to another elevator and punched the button for the first floor.

"How many elevators do you have?" asked Mariam.

"There are four," said Alex. "We have our private elevator. The elevator we came down in only goes to the third floor and can only be used to come to the penthouse apartment. No one can use it without being accompanied by one of my employees. There are two other elevators for everyone else. They do not go to the penthouse."

Mariam did not say anything as the door opened on the first floor. Alex led the way out of the elevator. Mariam looked around. On one side of the hall, there was a beauty shop and down from it was a barbershop. At the end of the hall, she saw a sign saying, "Children's Day Care." On the other side of the hall was a cafeteria-style restaurant.

Alex led her toward the restaurant.

"I'm not really hungry," said Mariam.

"I'm not either," said Alex. "We can get a cup of coffee, and you can meet Andre. He runs the place. If you ever want to order anything from him, you can just call, and it will be delivered to the penthouse."

They went in, and the hostess smiled and greeted Alex. "Hello, Lynn, is Andre here?" asked Alex.

Lynn led the way to a table. "Yes, he is, Mr. Avorn. I'll tell him you are asking for him. I'll send Wanda over for your order." She handed them menus.

"We just want coffee," said Alex, handing back the menus. Lynn took the menus and left with a smile. Wanda was there with coffee almost instantly. She was followed by Andre.

"Alex, it's good to see you back!" exclaimed Andre. Alex stood and shook his hand.

"I'd like you to meet my wife, Mariam," said Alex with a big smile.

"You're married?" exclaimed Andre with a big smile for Mariam. "Congratulations." He shook Alex's hand again. "This calls for something stronger than coffee. Wanda, bring Alex and Mariam a bottle of champagne," called Andre.

"You can take it with you and drink it later when you are alone," said Andre.

Wanda came to the table, bringing a bottle of champagne. Andre took it and handed it to Alex. "Enjoy, my friend. I wish you and your beautiful wife many happy years together," said Andre.

"Thanks, Andre," said Alex.

"Thank you," said Mariam with a smile for Andre.

"Would you join us for a coffee?" asked Alex.

"I am needed in the kitchen," said Andre. "You bring the lovely Mariam back for a meal, real soon, on the house."

"Thanks, Andre, we will take you up on it soon. I've already told Mariam how great the food is here," said Alex.

"It's the best in town," agreed Andre.

With another smile and congratulations, Andre left to take care of the kitchen.

Mariam smiled at Alex. "It's like you have your own town here in your building," she said.

"You have only seen a small part of it. I had help getting the building how I wanted it. My grandfather started it, then my father added on to it. I changed it and got rid of some of the renters and worked on having businesses opened that complimented each other. It's been a work in progress. You ready to go look around some more?" asked Alex. Mariam nodded, and Alex took the bottle of champagne in one hand and Mariam's hand in the other and led the way.

When they were back in the elevator, Alex explained further about the building, "The second floor has the spa and a ladies' boutique." He held the elevator door open so she could glance out at the second floor, but they did not get out. "We can explore it later," said Alex. Mariam nodded as Alex let the doors close. "The third floor is Avorn Security; the fourth floor has offices. There are three lawyers and an accountant office there," said Alex. He pushed the button for the fifth floor.

"The fifth floor is the gym. It is divided into two sides. One is regular and easy-going, and the other is for the more intense workout. It is for the more serious physical workout." The doors opened on the fifth floor, and they stepped out and looked around. After a glance around, Alex led Mariam back into the elevator and pushed the door for the sixth floor.

"What's on this floor?" asked Mariam.

"This floor is divided into four apartments," said Alex.

Mariam looked at him in surprise. "Someone lives here?" she asked.

"Sometimes," agreed Alex. "I keep two of them available for emergencies. In case I need somewhere to take a client for safety reasons. If I have someone visiting from out of town, sometimes I let them use one of the apartments. The other two apartments are available for my agents to use if they need to."

They exited the elevator on the sixth floor, and Alex led her to another door. He opened the door, and there were stairs going up and down. Alex led the way up and used a key to open the door into the penthouse.

Mariam stepped into the penthouse and took a deep breath. She turned and looked at Alex, who was looking at her expectantly.

"Wow," she said. "Talk about change of lifestyle. It's going to take me a while to get used to this."

Alex set down the bottle of champagne and took her into his arms.

"I know, and like I told you, we also have a house. We can split our time between the two," he said. He drew her close and kissed her.

"Let's put the champagne in the fridge and save it for later," said Mariam.

"Okay," agreed Alex, doing as she suggested.

The phone rang as Alex started back to Mariam.

"Alex," said Brenda. "I was looking at the report about the police officer from Madison who was killed in Mercy. The strange thing is he has the same last name as the lawyer who has been trying to get in touch with Mariam about the insurance money."

"I see," said Alex.

"I also checked on the life insurance. Mariam's dad had taken out a two-hundred-and-fifty-thousand-dollar policy on himself and his wife and each of the children," said Brenda.

"So, this whole thing may have nothing to do with witches. Someone is using the witch hunters to get rid of people so they can collect their insurance," said Alex.

"It looks that way," agreed Brenda. Alex told Mariam everything he had just learned.

Mariam paled. "We need to warn Darrin. They may be after him, too!" she exclaimed.

Alex nodded. "Brenda is there any way we can get in touch with Mark or Darrin?" he asked.

"Mark just called. He is on Skype. Turn on your computer," said Brenda.

Alex hurried over to his computer and turned it on. It came on instantly, and he connected to Skype.

Mark and Darrin were sitting in front of a computer smiling at them.

"Hey, Sis," said Darrin, grinning at Mariam as she sat beside Alex.

"Darrin, are you alright?" asked Mariam.

"I'm fine, thanks to Mark," said Darrin.

"What happened?" asked Alex.

"One of the guys in our platoon tried to knock Darrin out. I saw him and knocked him out instead. He is in the military prison awaiting trial. He confessed to being paid by his uncle to kill Darrin. It seems his brother and sister were in on it, too. The uncle was your dad's lawyer. He had a nephew on the police force, and the lawyer convinced them they could use their sister to pretend she was Mariam and collect the insurance money for the whole family. They stood to collect a million dollars. They used the witch hunters to cover their tracks. The military contacted the FBI, and they are on their way to Madison to arrest the uncle, sister, and the other nephew," Mark stopped to draw a breath.

"They won't be able to arrest the other nephew,"

said Alex. "He is dead. He was killed by the police in Mercy when he set fire to the bookstore Mariam has been working in."

"Is Mariam alright?" asked Darrin.

"She is fine. We had already left. We are married, and I brought her home with me," said Alex.

"You are married?" said Darrin and Mark with big grins.

"Yes, we are," said Mariam with a smile.

"All right," said Mark and Darrin, giving each other high fives.

Alex and Mariam smiled at each other and then looked back at their brothers.

Mark and I were hoping you two would fall in love," said Darrin.

"I love him very much," said Mariam.

"I love your sister with all my heart," said Alex.

"Are you sure you guys are alright?" asked Mariam.

"We are fine. I'm glad we finally discovered what was going on," said Darrin.

"Mariam wants to put the insurance money on the house into an account for you for when you return to the states," said Alex.

"You can open an account for me, but you split all of the insurance money down the middle. You can use your half to open up college funds for any possible children you have," said Darrin. "If I meet my match, I can do the same thing with my share. I think Mom and Dad would approve."

"What a wonderful idea. Yes, Mom and Dad would approve," agreed Mariam.

"We have to go," said Mark. "We have used up all

of our time. You guys take care of each other. We will be in touch when we can."

"Bye, Sis, love you," said Darrin.

"I love you, too. You and Mark stay safe," said Mariam.

"Congratulations, Alex," said Mark. "I'm looking forward to getting to know my new sister."

The connection faded, and Mariam turned into Alex's arms.

"Is it really over?" she asked.

"It would seem so," said Alex, holding her close. "I'll have my lawyer look into the insurance and make sure your dad's lawyer hasn't done any damage to the accounts."

"Thanks, I wouldn't know where to start," said Mariam.

"I think I will call those FBI agents we talked to and see if I can find out if they have arrested your dad's lawyer, yet," said Alex.

Mariam wandered into the kitchen in search of something to drink while Alex called his lawyer and told him to find out what was happening with the insurance.

Alex then called Agent Hatch and asked him if he knew anything about the case. Then he joined Mariam in the kitchen. "Agent Hatch said the agents in Madison have the lawyer and his niece under arrest. He couldn't tell me anything else because it is an ongoing case," said Alex. "My lawyer will take care of the insurance company and let us know what to expect from them."

"Good," said Mariam. "Can we forget about all of this and get back to our honeymoon. My guardian angel says it's about time, and you always need to listen to Love's Voice."

"Yes, Ma'am," agreed Alex as he drew her close and prepared to obey.

THE END

Dear reader,

We hope you enjoyed reading *Love's Voice*. Please take a moment to leave a review, even if it's a short one. Your opinion is important to us.

Discover more books by Betty McLain at

https://www.nextchapter.pub/authors/betty-mclain

Want to know when one of our books is free or discounted? Join the newsletter at

http://eepurl.com/bqqB3H

Best regards,

Betty McLain and the Next Chapter Team

The story continues in:
Love's Helper by Betty McLain

To read the first chapter for free, please head to:
https://www.nextchapter.pub/books/loves-helper

ABOUT THE AUTHOR

With five children, ten grandchildren, and six great-grandchildren, I have an extremely busy life, but reading and writing have always been a large and enjoyable part of my life. I've been writing since I was young. I wrote stories in notebooks and kept them private. They were all handwritten because I was unable to type. We lived in the country, and I had to do most of my writing at night. My days were busy helping with my brothers and sister. I also helped Mom with the garden and canning food for our family. Even though I was tired, I still managed to get my thoughts down on paper at night.

When I married and began raising my family, I continued writing my stories while helping my children through school and then transitioning into their own lives and families. My sister was the only one to read my stories. She was very encouraging. When my youngest daughter started college, I decided to go to college myself. I had already completed my GED and only had to take a class to prepare for my college entrance tests. I passed with flying colors and even managed to get a partial scholarship. I took computer classes to learn typing. The English and literature classes helped me polish my stories.

I found that public speaking was not for me. I was much more comfortable with the written word, but researching and writing the speeches was helpful. I was able to use those skills to build a story.

I finished college with an associate degree and a 3.4 GPA. I earned several awards, including the President's List, Dean's List, and Faculty List. My school experience helped me gain more confidence with writing. I want to thank my college English professor for boosting my confidence with writing by telling me that I had a good imagination. She said I told an interesting story. My daughter, who is an excellent writer and has published many books, convinced me to publish some of my stories. She used her experience self-publishing to publish my stories for me. The first time I held one of my books and looked at my name on it as the author, I was proud. It was well received, which encouraged me to continue writing and publishing. I have been building my library of books since then. I've also written and illustrated several children's books.

Being able to type my stories opened up a whole new world for me. Access to a computer helped me research anything I needed to know and expanded my ability to keep writing my books. Joining Facebook and making friends all over the world expanded my outlook considerably. I was able to understand many different lifestyles and incorporate them into my stories.

Ever heard the saying, "Watch out what you say, and don't make the writer mad. You may end up in a book being eliminated." Well, it is true. All of life is there to stimulate your imagination. It is fun to develop a story and to watch it come alive in your mind. When I get started, the stories almost write themselves; I just have to get all of it down as the ideas come to me before they're gone.

I love knowing that the stories I have written are being read and enjoyed by others. It is awe-inspiring to look at the books and think, "I wrote that."

I look forward to many more years of creating and distributing my stories, and I hope the people reading my books are looking forward to reading them just as much as I enjoy writing them.

Love's Voice
ISBN: 978-4-86752-095-6
Mass Market

Published by
Next Chapter
1-60-20 Minami-Otsuka
170-0005 Toshima-Ku, Tokyo
+818035793528

20th July 2021